MW01613505

ALL THAT GLITTERS

Matestone Guardians #2

BEE MURRAY

Copper!
Happy Reading!
♡ Bee Murray

Copyright © 2021 by Bee Murray

All rights reserved.

No part of this book may be reproduced in any form or by any electronic or mechanical means, including information storage and retrieval systems, without written permission from the author, except for the use of brief quotations in a book review.

Cover: Dexpress Covers

Editing: Girls Heart Edits

Formatting: Inked Imagination Author Services

A lot of people dedicate books to their friends or family. And I love my friends and my family. They are everything to me. But this book is dedicated to my leggings -- the only thing that has consistently kept my ass in line for this entire pandemic year. Stretchy pants for the win. It's been a long year.

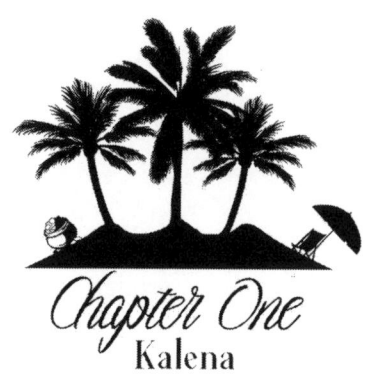

Chapter One
Kalena

"Helll-ooo! New girl! I've got a Blood of Satan, a Broken Heart Zombie Mai Tai, and some Pink Silk Panties over here for table nine. Braylie or whatever your name is? Are you working or are you flirting?!" I shouted, struggling to be heard over the din of the thumping house music and screaming women.

The server in question was new, and we were already getting off to a poor start. She glared at me viciously from where she was perched, practically in the lap of one of our regulars, Rudy.

She flipped her long brown hair over her shoulder, dragged a finger along Rudy's jawline, and then reluctantly peeled herself away and stalked over to grab her tray from me in a huff.

"Don't let Seamus catch you doing that, girl. You'll be out on your ass so fast you won't know what hit you. And Rudy? The man is flat broke, shares a den with at least three other foxes, and has some… peculiar… tastes. He's pretty, but… Not. Worth it." I warned her.

She just scowled some more and stomped off. I

couldn't be sure, but I was fairly certain I heard some mutterings of "Bitch" and "Worthless Witch" under her breath as she flounced back out onto the club floor.

"Oh, Ice Queen strikes again! That one is so not going to tip you out, *a stór*, and you better watch your back or she's gonna claw you in the dark corners. Something tells me Miss Braylie doesn't like to be told no."

My eyes rolled so far back into my head I thought they might get stuck, but I turned around and smiled anyway. Belfast. My favorite dancer in this godforsaken shithole. He was leaning over the bar, pouring himself a shot of Bushmills and grinning like an imp.

"Hey, get out of there! You know Seamus is itching for a reason to make an example out of me. Pay for your drinks like everyone else, asshole." I swatted at him with my bar towel but spared him a rueful smile.

There's something about Belfast that makes a girl want to forget all the rules. And I mean *all of them.*

A gentle dusting of gold glitter covered the surface of the bar as he straightened up and perched himself on a bar stool.

"Seamus won't lay a hand on you, *a stór*, for sure and certain. I won't allow it," he promised.

I wished I could believe him. His brilliant green eyes twinkled as he threw back the shot and smacked his lips in satisfaction. A little drop of whiskey rested on the corner of his lip, and I had a strange desire to lean across and lick it off.

I busied myself with wiping down the bar again to resist.

"If he so much as looks at you wrong, I'll fuck him up for you!"

I looked up and stared at him for a long moment before cackling so loudly several of the patrons at the bar

2

actually moved to get away from me. *Top-notch customer service here.*

The night had been shit thus far, and I needed this laugh.

It wasn't that Belfast was incapable of fighting. The man was scrappy as hell and had more muscles than any person really should have. He practically rippled when he walked. It was borderline ridiculous.

But Belfast was muscular, like a greyhound. Lean, fast, strong, prone to intense bursts of movements followed by leisurely naps and relaxation.

Our boss Seamus was a goblin, and that meant he was small, burly, strong, and vicious. Goblins rarely lost in a brawl against their own kind, much less against mystical greyhound-like glitter creatures.

Belfast was lucky. So I was certain he would get one punch in. But even a Leprechaun could run out of luck, and I couldn't see a way to victory against Seamus unless he drugged him beforehand or managed a KO shot in one. In all likelihood, it would be the last punch of his strange, glittery life.

"Should I be offended, *a stór,*" Belfast frowned at me.

I struggled to stop laughing, but the pout on Belfast's otherwise perfect face was reminding me of a child who didn't get a candy they wanted and it was making me giggle.

Pull yourself together, Kalena. He's basically your only friend. Even if you do sometimes fantasize about biting his perfect ass and... other things. Ugh.

My bar towel fell to the ground and I ducked down and pulled myself together. By the time I popped back up, my game face was back on. I reached across the sticky bar and grabbed his hand.

"You're the sweetest guy around here, Belfast. You're

my favorite, and I appreciate that you've got my back. Just… ignore me. I'm all kinds of weird tonight. My magic is itching to get out."

Belfast looked skeptical.

He crossed his arms over his perfect, golden, glitter-covered chest and arched an eyebrow at me.

A worried feeling started in my gut that maybe I had actually offended him. With a heavy sigh, I dug in my pocket and withdrew my thin cash clip. I pulled a bedraggled $10 bill out and waved it at the security witch before placing it in the register.

Grabbing the Bushmills, I poured him a double shot and slid it across the bar.

"Do you believe me now, my glittery friend?" I asked, batting my eyelashes at him and striking a pose.

He glared at me for another minute before breaking into a huge grin. Grabbing the shot, he tossed it back without hesitation.

"Overjoyed beyond all comprehension, beautiful. Now, tell me, who should I pull on stage tonight. You've seen all of them come in. Anyone I should pay attention to?"

I lifted my head and surveyed the sea of people crowding the dance floor and performance areas. We were packed.

Lucky Charmz Club was the number one place to see and be seen in Las Vegas right now. All the blogs called us 'the hottest little dive you've never heard of' and yet we never lacked for customers. Humans, as far as the eye can see in the audience. *Bless their little hearts.*

Lucky Charmz was the only bar and strip club on the Vegas Strip with a 100% supernatural staff. Not that the humans knew any better. They were just here to see bodies on display and get drunk. An evening to forget their lives and responsibilities to indulge in hedonistic pleasures. If you told them that their favorite dancer was actually a selkie, they'd probably assume you drugged their drink.

The opening bars of the main event music sounded throughout the crowded room and a cheer went up from our patrons.

Belfast tapped on the bar impatiently and snapped me back to reality. I pointed towards a smaller gaggle of women sitting at one of the cheaper reserved tables.

"Blue sash, blinking balls on her tiara, kind of mousy looking? Looks like her friends are attaching condoms to her veil? That one tipped me $20 for a white wine spritzer, looks distinctly uncomfortable, and I overheard her saying she thought all the dancers tonight were breathtaking, but you in particular."

Belfast nodded solemnly. "Done, my lady. I'll bring her up for the 2nd chair dance portion. Anyone else?"

I pointed out another three or four women and Belfast made note of each of them.

Belfast wasn't like a lot of the other dancers here. He never got jaded. Unlike the succubi and incubi, he didn't *need* this job to feed or survive, he just loved to dance and make people feel special. Often that meant singling out people who were often overlooked at a place like this. Everything else, even the money, was a secondary concern to him.

It's one reason I liked him so much. The other reason was because I knew his secret.

He was pretty tight-lipped about his past, but one night I'd got him drunk and he admitted he was a Leprechaun, complete with a pot of gold and everything.

He swore me to secrecy that night and gave me some bullshit story about hiding from his powerful family and how much he loved to dance because it was the only time he truly felt free. Yadda yadda. The same dancer talk I'd heard a thousand times before.

It was probably bullshit, but I still felt special that he shared it with me.

"I bet you all my tips for the next hour that Blue Balls is going to drag you into a private room after your chair dance with her!" I smirked at him knowingly.

That's the problem with making people feel special. Sometimes, they feel *too special* and they take liberties.

It happened every shift without fail.

Usually a cheeky bridesmaid or bachelorette would get it in their pretty little heads to take charge, and they would always try it with Belfast. The divorce party gals were notorious for it, too.

Belfast would always politely decline and then they would get fussy with him and he would have to use magic to get them to go away. Night after night, he would wait for me at the bar while I cleaned and regale me with the stories of the crazy shit that happened in the private dance booths.

I'd be lying if I said it wasn't one of my favorite parts of my job.

Belfast squinted and scrutinized the woman for a long moment before turning back to me.

"Too easy. I don't want you to just give me your hard-earned cash, I want to earn it properly," he teased. "I'll raise the stakes. I bet you I can get all four of them in a private dance *and* buy me a bottle of whiskey as a tip. If I fail, I will give you a piece of Leprechaun gold of your very own. If I win, I get to pull you on stage tonight for Midnight Mass and you can be the envy of all the women in here."

I froze. As much as I may have fantasized about Belfast

dancing on me like he did our patrons, the idea of it actually happening made me break out in the world's most unsexy sweat. Being on display? Having to sit on the chair on stage while Belfast and the others dipped, ground, and dove around me while everyone watched?

Uh. No thank you. Do not want. I'm really more of a *private* dance kind of person.

There's an excellent reason I work *behind* the bar, not on top of it. I've had a lifelong fear of being on stage.

But Leprechaun gold intrigued me. That was a helluva bet. He knew it, too. I'd been itching for a piece of that Leprechaun gold for ages and four private dances plus a bottle of our top shelf whiskey would mean a lot more money coming in tonight than Belfast usually had.

"Fine," I said carefully. Leprechauns are part of the Fae, so any bets made are legally binding. The phrasing had to be exact.

"But! As proof of the four dances, you have to be able to tell me all of their names. In the order in which you danced for them. You can tell Donovan when you go back there. Gargoyles can't forget things and he has a thing for you so you know he will help you remember if you promise to buy him a drink later."

Belfast grinned ear to ear and stuck his hand out in agreement. His entire body seemed to shimmer just a little more. It was probably a trick of the lights, but I still took his hand with some hesitance. He shook it soundly before leaning over the bar again to press a soft kiss to my cheek.

"I've been looking forward to dancing for you for a long time, *a stór*. This is one bet I will *not* lose."

A small tingle of awareness pooled in my belly as I watched him saunter off, his perfectly biteable ass swaying in those skintight shorts.

Belfast. Man of mystery, glitter, gold, and... glutes. *I*

hate to see him leave, but I love to watch him go. I wonder what it would be like to see him com… NO. Focus, Kalena.

The next wave of screeching bachelorettes came through the door and I reluctantly looked away from Belfast's fine ass and pasted a professional, semi-friendly smile on my face. Working on autopilot, I had the blenders started and the shot glasses primed before the first gaggle made it to the bar.

When Lucky Charmz got busy, there was a certain rhythm to it all, a predictability in the chaos that I found almost comforting. If you had asked me ten years ago if I was interested in spending long hours making fruity drinks for screaming women with glowing plastic dicks attached to their headbands, I would have tried to hex you.

Yet, here we are.

There's no shame in being a bartender. Not for humans, anyway. Bartending is a perfectly legitimate and honorable line of work.

Unless you are the daughter of Daymian and Terrica Montague of the Bay City Montagues.

Then… it's a big fucking embarrassment. To them.

Our home coven actually had a meeting about it, delicately asking if I might consider using a different name so they wouldn't be brought down by my shameful choices. *Selfish, narcissistic pricks.*

It's not like I'd planned for this.

No kid dreams of being a poorly paid, often-harassed bartender at a paranormal strip joint run by the kingpin of Las Vegas' very own goblin mafia.

Ten years ago, I'd had a *plan*. I was going to graduate from St. Basil's Academy with enough skills to make a respectable living as a hedge witch or a dream interpreter. I've always had an affinity for plants, and my family line is known for dream walking. There were options. They weren't glamorous, but it was honest work that sparked my spirit.

Back then, I'd even let myself get excited about it. I'd dreamed about what my life might be like, the people I might meet, and the gardens I would rejuvenate.

Those dreams were the only thing that sustained me while I struggled to hide the other side of me, the side that no one could know about. My secret shame.

Secrets don't stay secret forever in the world of witches. As much as we try, we can never fully hide things from some people. When the news about my parentage broke, it was an enormous scandal and my parents were mortified. They were even sanctioned by their coven for hiding the truth from them. No one said a word to them about hiding the truth from me.

For twelve years, they hid the fact that my biological father wasn't the man who had taken me to the park and eaten dinner across from me every day for my entire life. He was a koala shifter that my mom had a fling with in college.

Which made me half witch, half koala. It was a lot to take in.

One night, while the scandal was raging full force and the Council was talking about sanctions for my parents, I overheard them talking about sending me away to a cousin-coven in Alaska or somewhere less visible.

That's when I realized I was truly on my own in this world. They were only looking out for themselves.

I was fifteen.

The very next day, I quit school before they could throw me out and struck out on my own. My parents never questioned it. They just let me go.

It's been years since we spoke and now and then I wonder what they told their precious friends when asked about me. Probably that I died.

"Yo, birdbrain, I need a white wine, three Hanky Pankys, a Liquid Viagra, two Angel Tits, a Screaming Orgasm, and a Suck, Bang, and Blow. NOW." Braylie slapped the order on the bar and scowled at me.

Someone knows how to hold a grudge.

"What's in a Screaming Orgasm?" one of the cute young things waiting in line screeched loudly, her friends in the matching "Chelsee's Bride Squad" sashes all erupted in high-pitched giggles.

They reminded me of a flock of hissing geese. Pink, hissing geese. *I hate geese.*

"Someone call for a Screaming Orgasm?" Belfast appeared out of nowhere and set the entire flock of women at the bar off into maniacal giggles and cackles.

I rolled my eyes at him as he worked the crowd. If handling people was an art form, Belfast was a true master. He flirted effortlessly with whoever was in his line of sight and came across as both friendly and approachable, while remaining entirely aloof.

The house lights flickered, and I looked at my watch. Five minutes to show time.

Grabbing a water bottle from the fridge under the bar, I lobbed it at Belfast and pointed towards the stage.

"Your fans await, Belfast. And we," I gestured towards the giggling women around me, "We need to see that fine ass of yours sliding down the pole."

The surrounding women giggled even more and nodded in agreement.

"As you wish, oh beautiful Bar Mistress" Belfast executed a beautiful courtly bow and then darted away.

The girls grabbed their drinks and hurried back to their tables. There was a certain anticipatory energy in the room that was almost as intoxicating as the alcohol I served. My magic danced through my veins and I let the adrenaline rush crash over me, an almost palpable caress over my skin.

When the lights dimmed, deafening shrieks rose from the audience. A burly man in an atrocious green fedora swaggered to the microphone on the stage and raised his hand for silence.

"What time is it?" He called out, holding the microphone out to the crowd.

"Time to get lucky!" the crowd screeched back.

As much as my job usually sucked, I secretly loved Saturday nights at Lucky Charmz. It's the only night we hold Midnight Mass - the (patented) hedonistic display of dancing and debauchery that made us famous.

The emcee continued going through his announcements and opening schitck, but I could feel the energy in the room pulsing.

A few months ago, Seamus had hired an Empath witch and set them up with a mirror so they could amplify emotional responses. It was a brilliant, albeit illegal, business move. Having a witch mirror the excitement and shine it back on the crowd would ensure everyone had a great time and people who were having a good time spent more money.

I leaned on my elbows on the bar, comforted by the anonymity of the darkness, and settled in to watch.

Clouds of smoke filled the runway and one by one, the dancers filed out. Hoods covered their faces from view.

The audience shrieked even louder.

Each of the dancers lowered their hoods and struck a

pose when their stage name was announced. The men of Lucky Charmz come in every shape, size, and species, and Seamus prided himself on having something for every taste. There were certainly a few who met my specifications. *Like a certain golden Leprechaun, maybe?*

Spending my Saturday night watching beautiful people dance wasn't the worst thing I could do with my time. It distracted me from the fact that I was alone, broke, and trapped in a meaningless job. *Being surrounded by abs does that to you.*

"Am I paying you to drool over the staff or am I paying you to prepare drinks, Ms. Montague? Pray tell, remind me," Seamus' bitter voice slid down my spine and I straightened immediately, turning to face my boss with trepidation.

"My apologies, sir. Won't happen again."

I took special care to lower my eyes to the floor and use a meek voice. Seamus was famous for his quick temper and I had learned how to handle his frequent mercurial mood swings the hard way.

"See that it does not, Kalena. Or I'm afraid we'll have to discuss this in my office."

I fought back a grimace and nodded in agreement. Many people went into Seamus' office…. Few of them came out unharmed.

The prevailing opinion among the staff was that he had a Hellmouth in there and fed those who displeased him into it to appease his demon friends. If I didn't know better, I'd say it was a legit theory.

But the truth was far less fantastical and more sinister.

Goblins are skilled information-brokers, and Seamus was no exception. You don't get to his position in the organized crime world without a certain set of skills.

It was a well-known fact that Seamus traded in secrets as much as he traded in flesh. Those that went into his office were often subjected to truth serums and truth crystals until they spilled their deepest, darkest secrets to him.

He rarely killed them. They stopped being useful when they were dead. He just blackmailed them until they wished they were dead. It was enough of a threat that I vowed to stay wary a long time ago and never cross him if I could help it.

I'd hidden my dual nature this long and I'd be damned before I let a slimy old goblin hold it over my head or worse - take an interest in it.

Seamus sat at the bar for the rest of the Midnight Mass, watching his staff with a critical eye and jotting down notes on a small tablet.

By the time the set ended and the crowds swarmed my bar again, my anxiety felt like ants crawling all over my skin and I just wanted to get through my shift and escape.

I was on my best behavior. I laughed at the ridiculous jokes, endured the casually offensive lines offered by the few men in attendance, and made more ridiculous phallic-named drinks than I thought was possible.

Each time Belfast tried to corner me between sets, I brushed him off, casting nervous glances at where Seamus sat frowning at everyone.

This job sucked, but it was the only one I had.

If Seamus told Belfast to fuck off and get out tonight, he'd be ok. The man was a Leprechaun, for goodness' sake. He had resources.

But not me.

If Seamus fired me, I would end up losing my shitty trailer and probably living in my trash heap of a car and praying to the Moon Goddess, herself, that I could find menial labor somewhere. There are very few options out there for an Academy dropout without coven support.

The last call bell rang at 2:00 am and I heaved a sigh of relief.

Seamus finally left the bar area and retreated to his office, slamming the door shut. Cabs were called for our drunken clientele and dancers sat out at the tables, counting their tips.

I hurried through my closeout duties, eager to get out. Seamus' close attention made me uneasy and the exhaustion of the night was catching up with me.

I shoved a handful of bills at the security witch and practically ran out the door.

After the club took their cut, I had made a measly $100 for the night.

I walked out to my car, trying to do math in my head to figure out how I could afford to eat after I paid for my gas, electric, and water. *Should have been an electro-witch. That would have been helpful.*

My car was old and not very efficient, and the commute back to my tiny little trailer was an hour and a half. It was going to be a tight week. I sighed.

"Wait up, buttercup!" Belfast called out. He hurried to catch up with me, holding the stage door for me and then closing it carefully behind us.

I toyed with my keys and walked towards the brown Ford that had been my mainstay for years.

"Good night, Belfast, I gotta go. I'm dead on my feet."

"You won!" He called out behind me.

His words stopped me in my tracks. *Won? Really?*

"Come over here," he grabbed my forearm and maneuvered me behind the dumpster, facing the driveway. "Cameras don't extend this far, I checked."

"That's what every woman wants to hear when being

manhandled by a shirtless man in the dead of the night. Really, reassuring." I said dryly.

To his credit, Belfast looked concerned. "I would never hurt you, *a stór*. Never." He vowed fiercely.

With a pained expression on his face, he pressed his hand against his heart and pulled outward, a small string of golden light following behind his hand. I froze, fascinated despite myself.

When enough of the light was pulled out, he stopped and snapped his fingers and the golden light transformed into a beautiful rainbow. A neon green paint bucket covered in vinyl show stickers appeared next to the dumpster. It took me a minute to process what I was seeing. Gold glittered from the top.

Holy shit! This is it! A Leprechaun's pot of gold!

"Uh, your pot of gold is not what I thought it would look like," I ventured cautiously. I craned my neck to see inside the bucket, curiosity getting the best of me. *Maybe he's like a... clearance Leprechaun?*

"Choose a piece of gold, Kalena. You've earned it," Belfast's voice was strained, as if holding the gold here was physically challenging for him. *Don't have to tell me twice!*

I shoved my hand into the bucket and swirled my fingers around before grabbing a piece at random. I didn't stop to look at it, I just shoved it into my pocket before he could change his mind.

"Got one!" I said and backed up towards my car. "Have a good night!"

I waved, but Belfast didn't answer. A flash of gold light in the dark was the only sign that he was even still there.

The ominous creak of my car door echoed in the quiet night air as I slid inside and started the engine. She purred to life after only a few hiccups, and I sent up a silent prayer of thanks.

Nosing out of the narrow driveway, I yawned and headed towards the highway. The coin in my pocket felt warm and comforting, and a strange sense of premonition fell over me as I continued to drive.

It was a weird night all around. I was looking forward to passing out in my tiny little trailer soon.

Chapter Two
Belfast

Goosebumps appeared on my bare arms and chest, but I barely felt the cold. I just stood out in the middle of the parking lot and watched until her tail lights disappeared. Giving Kalena a piece of my gold had been impulsive. If my father had seen me so casually distributing my treasure, he'd be apoplectic with rage. "Leprechauns keep the gold, we don't give it away!" he would have roared.

Kalena did that to me. She had an energy about her that was unlike anything else I had ever encountered. It was bold, chaotic, and vibrant. She practically pulsed with restrained power. *Gods, Kalena was something else.*

Everything about her drew me in. From her long purple hair to her soft curves and strikingly expressive hazel eyes.

Basking in her energy was addicting. *She* was addicting. I just wished I knew why I was so drawn to her.

"You're mooning after her like a schoolboy, you fool," I muttered to myself and kicked a rock across the parched earth of the parking lot.

I shrugged my shoulders in defeat and walked off

towards the club building. She was already gone. There was no point in waiting around any longer. *Another night, another pile of money. Whatever.*

Seamus was nowhere to be seen by the time I had collected my duffel bag and personal effects. The goblin was a cagey bastard, and I always expected him to be lurking in dark corners and shadowed hallways.

"Good night, Belfast! Sweet dreams!" Braylie jumped down from the bar and sidled up to me, gripping my arm in a strange sort of one-armed hug.

I shook her off in disgust and looked down at her through narrowed eyes.

Braylie was a groundhog shifter with surprisingly poor survival instincts. *Time to fix that.*

The sad, desperate little creature had a lot of gall to treat Kalena so poorly, and I was tired of it. When she brushed her arm against mine again, I snapped.

"I do not want you. How many ways do I need to explain this to you?"

My voice boomed through the cavernous room, and the remaining staff members stopped talking to stare at us.

Braylie looked like she was about to cry. Her bottom lip stuck out and quivered.

"You would do well to learn your place, shifter. Learn to be professional or I'll make sure you never work here again," I growled at her, pushing past her shaking form and stomping towards the door.

A part of me wanted to turn around and comfort her, but I stayed the course. This woman had intentionally been badgering Kalena all night, and that didn't even count the rumors I had heard in the dressing room.

The ridiculous woman would likely spend the rest of the weekend wondering if she had lost her new job and talking like that certainly wouldn't make me any friends among Braylie and the rest of the cocktail staff, but... I didn't care. If they couldn't manage even the most basic levels of politeness to a colleague, I couldn't be bothered either.

Actions had consequences. I, of all people, was acutely aware of that.

This time when I stepped outside, the cool night air was welcome on my skin. I yawned and then hurried over to the designated portal area.

Portals used to be so simple. You took your light, or whatever portal apparatus you used, told it where you wanted to go and you, more or less, got there.

But modern technology and humans' steadfast refusal to accept the supernaturals living all around them had made calling a portal more complicated. Now there was the added irritation of protection runes, mathematical calculations, and even weather reports. *What is the world coming to when a Leprechaun can't even call a rainbow without a fucking weather forecast?*

I pulled out my rainbow light and cast my destination runes.

"Gods, I miss the good old days," I yawned again, double-checking the runes before popping in the center of the rainbow portal.

"Home again, home again, jiggity jig."

With a flash of blinding light and the all-too-familiar pull in my core, I stepped out of my rainbow and into my top-floor condo. The lights of the Las Vegas strip glittered in the distance. On a clear day, the view from my floor-to-ceiling windows stretched for miles.

The condo was luxurious, and the view was top notch, but sometimes, when I stood on the balcony and really looked, all I could see was the desolation of the desert.

This was a land of extremes. It was oppressively hot

during the day and bitterly cold at night. It was nothing like the brilliant green rolling hills and lush, waterlogged forests of my homeland.

A sudden, intense feeling of homesickness struck me and I sat down hard on the designer sofa. All the money, all the gold, all the magic in the world didn't make up for the fact that I had no proper home anymore, and aside from my sister, no real family ties, either.

My existence was a solitary one, banished to live in this strange parallel existence with the humans, the supernatural world, and Faery.

It was daunting and lonely.

Almost as if on cue, the small golden box on my coffee table vibrated. Similar to human cell phones, the Fae had developed what they referred to as "inter-dimensional conversation boxes" for contact between the planes. Only three people had the code to mine, and none of them ever called just to chat.

With much trepidation, I pushed the receiver button and waited while it scanned a hologram of me to project. I thought, rather belatedly, that I should have put on a robe or something over my dance shorts. Oh, well. Clothing was highly overrated.

"Brother!" my sister Eimear's sweet voice echoed out of the box and my heart rate slowed. "Brother, it is so wonderful to see you! I hope you are in good health and excellent wealth amongst the humans?"

I smiled at Eimear's formality and relaxed against the couch. *At least this feels familiar.*

"Are you ruling the place yet, Your Highness?" I asked, matching her formality with a hand to my heart.

The exasperated look she gave me warmed my heart at the same time that it fed into my pervasive loneliness. She launched into an update of everything that had happened on the Hill and I settled in to listen, allowing the warmth and lilt of her voice to lull me into a strange sense of contentment.

Of all the people on this cursed planet, Eimear was one of my favorites.

The memory of the day they brought her to me for the first time still burned brightly in my mind. Mother and Da bustled into my playroom one day and announced they had brought me a sister.

Even though she wasn't a baby, she was still the tiniest, most delicate little thing I had ever seen. I called her my little bird, and from the moment I set eyes on her, I knew I would always be her protector.

As a child, Eimear was withdrawn and shy, preferring the company of the garden gnomes and pixies to her own kind.

Our parents never paid her any mind or celebrated her. She just... existed. It wouldn't surprise me in the slightest if I learned my mother picked her out of a catalogue because she wanted a daughter that day.

Where I was trained to one day take over for my father, Eimear was left to explore her arts, to read, and play.

They trained her to be an ornament, never once taking the time to train her to be a Queen. Her entire existence was centered on the knowledge that she would never, ever have to rule our Hill.... *until I left and they had no other choice.*

"I miss you, Eimear. Know that." I interrupted her, an acute sense of loneliness threatening to crush me.

"Shut up, you loon, and listen to me. Father is in a massive temper and you can take advantage of it if you play your cards right," she started, and then glanced over her shoulder to look at something.

I sat up and leaned forward, suddenly interested.

"The Anam Cara has been detected on the human

plane! It's the first time in 150 years or something that we got a read on it. There's a chance we could get it back!" she whispered excitedly.

My blood froze in my veins and I tried to remain calm.

Oh, shit.

My pulse and my mind were racing in a million different directions.

"The Anam Cara, are you sure? That's been lost for centuries." I tried to look skeptical and casually sipped my whiskey.

Eimear rolled her eyes and scoffed at my lack of excitement at her news. Leaning forward into the projector, she beckoned me closer.

"Odhran, it's real. It's the real deal. Father paid the energy workers well to be sure and they tested it and it's the same signature. If you were to retrieve such an artifact, dear brother, surely then you could come home? All of *Tír Na nÓg* would welcome you back with open arms! Father would be forced to reinstate you or lose the will of the people and we could go back to the way things were!"

I couldn't breathe. I managed a nod, not trusting myself to speak.

Thankfully, Eimear took my silence for plotting and squealed again in excitement. Each second of her mindless chatter bought me another second to process this information.

If the Anam Cara had been sensed, that meant that it had to have been removed from its hiding place. Which was impossible. Utterly impossible. *I would know.*

"I have to go, brother. But swear to me you will search for it. Bring home the Anam Cara if you can? Swear it, Odhran."

I smiled at her weakly. If only she knew how hard I planned to search for that damn piece of gold.

"I so swear, Your Highness," I tilted my head at her but she still glared.

"Do it formally, Odhran. So I know you aren't just jerking me around." she snipped.

I smiled and rolled my eyes. "Very well, I, Prince Odhran, First Heir of Leprechaun Hill do solemnly swear to you, Princess Eimear also of Leprechaun Hill, that I will not rest in my search for the Anam Cara."

Eimear squealed again and blew me a kiss. A flurry of movement behind her caused her to cover her conversation box and the link was severed.

I exhaled slowly and braced my elbows on my knees for a long moment. *Holy Golden Shitbuckets.*

Carefully, I got up and closed the drapes, double-checking all the windows and locks. Once satisfied, I pulled my gold to me and instructed each pot and each bucket to dump out on my floor one at a time. The only way the Anam Cara could have been sensed was if someone had taken it from *my* hiding place, and that was impossible.

150 years I had kept that stupid coin as a giant fuck off to my father. It couldn't just... disappear. I would know.

Before long, my floor was carpeted wall to wall with coins made of every material known to man and Leprechauns. Gold, silver, bronze, copper, brass, hell - even a few made of bone, but no Anam Cara. *Fuck.*

My heart sank when I remembered my impulsive decision.

That could only mean one thing: by pure dumb luck, Kalena had taken possession of a priceless Leprechaun artifact and then not even know what to do with it.

Fear struck my heart at the idea of my former countrymen searching the Earthly plane for her to take their beloved gold back. They would do it by any means necessary, and that meant Kalena was in danger.

I waved my hand to send my gold back to my vault and grabbed a duffle bag. It was my fault she got involved in all of this, so it was my responsibility to keep her safe from whatever fresh hell I'd unleashed.

Moving on auto-pilot, I tossed belongings into the duffel and let myself concentrate on the unique signature of the Anam Cara and the soft, comforting chaos of Kalena.

"I'm coming for you, *a stór.*" I whispered as I cast my runes to begin my search.

Chapter Three
Kalena

The desert at night was creepy. Once you left the city lights and glamour behind, it was like driving on a different planet. The desert felt like an emptiness that surrounded you. A wildness that ebbed and flowed with immense energy.

Isolation. Darkness. Magic.

Creepy or not, I had grown to love it.

There was something... primal about living out here in the middle of god-forsaken-nowhere. This forgotten little corner of the planet was dirty and messed up and arguably dangerous, but it was my solace. My one place to be free.

My trailer wasn't anything special. It had a roof and a working door and a semi-working generator. But it was mine.

Out there, I was just another denizen of the desert who preferred isolation to company. No one asked questions. I learned the hard way it was better to stay away from people. If you didn't get close, they couldn't hurt you.

Normally, the drive back to my little corner of the desert was soothing. It was my way to decompress from yet another night of selling my soul for tips at Lucky Charmz or unpack whatever existential angst that was plaguing me.

But tonight was different. I felt uneasy and I couldn't put a finger on why.

My skin was crawling - like an electrical current humming just below the surface. It was more irritating than painful. The further I got away from the bright lights of Las Vegas and lost myself in the brilliant darkness of the Mojave, the more unsettled I felt.

Few cars passed me on the lone two-lane highway, and I set my cruise control and sucked down another gulp of piping hot tea from my battered travel mug. The citrusy notes of Earl Grey tickled my nose and the scalding hot liquid burned my throat, but it did nothing to solve the uneasy feeling that something was definitely... off.

My thoughts drifted to my shift tonight. No one stood out to me. New girl Braylie was obnoxious, and Seamus was predictably terrifying. Nothing out of the ordinary except a certain glittery, sexy Leprechaun and his pot of gold.

"Ugh, Belfast. What are you doing to me?" I groaned as I slammed my palm against the steering wheel. *He's not doing what you want him to be doing, that's for damn sure!*

There were approximately 200,000 reasons why I should never, ever date or mess around at my workplace. But every time I watched Belfast's arms wrapped around that pole, those ideas flew out of my head. Every last one. The flex of his muscles and the way he shimmered under the stage lights hypnotized me.

"Mmph." My long-suffering sigh sounded desperate, even for me.

Here's the thing. Lucky Charmz was known far and wide for extremely attractive dancers. Working there didn't make a person immune to that. We're supes. A lot of us were preternaturally gifted with elements of our appearance that attracts others to us. Being slightly attracted to your colleagues was just a hazard of working there.

But Belfast was different.

He was one of my precious few friends and crushing on your friends was always ill-advised.

"Pull it together, Kalena. It's just a crush. You can get over this the normal way. Just... hit up the human bar tomorrow night, find a nice looking cowboy and live out that weird country song. Save a horse, ride a goddamn cowboy."

My car was wholly uninterested in my pep talk and the idea of going to a bar to pick up a human felt vaguely distasteful. If you were craving something delicious, gourmet, and one-of-a-kind, but you decided at the last minute that fast food would do -- you wouldn't feel satisfied either.

Sorry, cowboys, but you can't compete with a jacked Leprechaun and his glittery pecs. *Mmph.*

Scrub and red rocks loomed in my headlights, and I tried to re-focus on the road in front of me.

The gold Belfast had given me was in my front shorts pocket. It had steadily gotten warmer the longer I drove until it almost burned me. I swerved the car slightly as I dug it out to look at it more closely.

Leprechaun gold.

I always thought it was a myth. But then again, Leprechauns and most of the Fae kept to themselves, so how was I supposed to know they hadn't all died out or killed themselves? *Exactly.*

"Is this your fault?" I asked the gold, accusingly.

It, being an inanimate object, didn't answer and I couldn't decide if that made me happy or sad. My experience examining pieces of gold was, arguably, limited. This piece seemed old. The gold was darker, tarnished by age. Words were engraved along the edges, but it wasn't a language I recognized. The squiggles and curls made me think of Elvish, or possibly even Faery.

I balanced the gold on my knee to take another swig of tea from my travel mug.

The coin seemed to glow slightly from one corner. I shifted so I could brace my knee against the steering wheel, licked my thumb, and rubbed the glowing corner industriously.

The glow intensified, and I felt a warmth flood through my entire body. The sensation started in the crown of my head and trickled downward. My magic perked up and swirled inside me, wanting to come out and answer whatever siren call this little coin had let out.

I shoved the coin roughly back into my pocket and took a reassuring gulp of my tea to calm my nerves. *Oh, helllll no.*

My training at St. Basil's might have been interrupted and my coven may have abandoned me, but I was still a witch. Kind of.

Inanimate objects containing magic that glowed were usually worth some caution. Everyone knew this. It's basic level shit.

Nervous and curious, I cruised down the highway and tried to think of what the coin might be. I almost didn't notice when the first twinge started. That persistent tickle underneath my skin, like ants trying to dig their way out. When it hit, I swerved in surprise and cursed when I drove up on the shoulder before pulling the car back onto the double-lane highway.

Panic rose within me and I tried to calm myself. "Hold it together, Kalena. It's just panic. You don't have to worry. You're safe. You're on your way home. You don't have to shift right now." I spoke aloud in soft, even tones - the way my mother had taught me. *Traitorous bitch though she may be.*

The feeling under my skin just intensified and sweat beaded on my forehead. My knuckles were white where I gripped the steering wheel tightly.

The desert spread out around me with nothing more than my headlights and the stars to light the way.

"Not here, please not here. We can wait until I get home. I'll let you out, I promise I will," I wheedled, addressing the most problematic side of myself.

If Belfast saw me like this, I bet he would think twice about being so nice to me. I looked unstable and wild as I muttered to myself, negotiating, berating, and pleading for just a little more time.

My breathing was short and shallow and my chest felt like fire. The panic combined with the denied shift was making my vision cloudy. Small bursts of hair popped up on my knuckles as my hands contorted.

A scream ripped through my throat as the rest of my body shuddered. Headlights gleamed in the darkness, shining directly at me, and fear suffocated me, closing my throat. My claw-like hands were still contorted, unable to grip the wheel. I jammed one elongated finger at the cruise control button and slammed my foot down on the brake, but nothing happened.

"I don't want to die," I sobbed as the car swerved again, directly onto the path of the oncoming vehicle. I swerved with my knee and the car careened in the opposite direction, towards the wide expanse of the desert.

My tired, junk heap of a car soared through the air and my body wrenched and contorted with the motion. The last thing I heard was the sound of a horn blaring frantically, followed by the sickening crunch of metal.

There was an explosion of pain followed by blissful darkness.

THE THICK SMELL of smoke woke me up followed immediately by the extreme pain in my entire body. I squirmed and tried to free myself but something had fallen on me, pinning me to the ground.

"Hang in there, Little Bit, I've almost got you," a gruff voice made me freeze in place. One hand was curled next to my face and I craned my neck to get a glance at it, praying to the Goddess above that it had shifted back to normal.

My claw-like hand was covered in blood and slightly mangled looking. A wave of nausea rose in me. I did not know if the man trying to rescue me was human or supe, but if I was still shifted, he was in for a big surprise.

I reached internally for my magic, hoping against hope that I would still have access to something -- but it lay dormant, unable, or unwilling to answer my call.

"Fuck," I whispered, tears tracking down my cheeks.

The heavy thing pinning my legs was carefully lifted off me and I let out a shaky breath of relief that was followed by a groan as my bones tried to sort themselves out.

"Can you move?" I saw two worn boots appear near my face as more debris was lifted off me and the pressure on my chest released slowly.

"I don't know," I croaked. My headache was something fierce, and it was hard to focus on anything. My entire brain felt like it was full of fog.

"Can you shift completely?" he asked again. A giant furry claw reached down into my line of sight to pick up another piece of gnarled metal and throw it out of the way.

I almost wept in relief. Another supe.

"What?," I blinked up at him curiously.

My savior grunted and then carefully scooped me up and pulled me out of the wreckage, cradling my broken form to his chest.

He was strong, that part was obvious, but he smelled like a pine forest after the rain and I buried my nose in his shirt and inhaled it again.

Along with the scene of pine, I caught the musky, earthy scent of a predator. A part of me wanted to be scared, but I buried my nose in his shirt again and I decided not to be. He smelled safe. And he rescued me. Surely, that had to count for something, right?

His long legs ate up the distance from the flaming wreckage to a shiny blue Mack truck parked on the side of the road.

The dim light from inside the cab made me wince and he murmured something before draping a warm, soft flannel over my head. It smelled like him and that calmed me instantly.

"I didn't know you were a shifter when I called for EMS," he said quietly, "They'll be here soon. If you can't shift back, I've got a first aid kit here that we can use if you would rather not be taken to the human hospital. Is there someone you want me to call?"

I blinked rapidly, trying to make sense of his words. Shifter? Someone to call? My mind was blank. Did I have someone he could call? I couldn't recall. I burrowed deeper into his flannel and shook my head, wincing at the motion. *Why couldn't I remember anything?*

He looked down at me with pity in his eyes and nodded heavily. "I can stabilize you, but you need to be treated."

I shook and trembled, tears welling up behind my eyes. The adrenaline left my body and pain and fear rushed in, along with the promise of blissful blackness.

"Hey, hey, Little Bit, stay with me! At least tell me your name?" his voice sounded muffled, like he was underwater.

"I don't r'member," I mumbled before I let the wave of darkness take me over once again.

Chapter Four
Frank

An unconscious shifter in the cab of my truck, a burning sedan along the side of the highway and me standing out here... in the middle of bumfuck nowhere.

In the words of my old Staff Sergeant: This was a Grade A, All-American Clusterfuck.

All we needed was a crazy ax murderer leaping out of the darkness to make this the plot of a B-grade horror movie.

I sighed heavily. It wasn't like there were that many alternate options.

Leaving her here was to condemn her to death, or worse, life as a human science experiment. She was obviously a supe and obviously in dire need of help.

Then there was the slight matter of my bear.

He had taken a very particular interest in her. The idea of something happening to her made him growl in my chest in a way that I did not have time to unpack.

"Who *are* you?" I looked down again at the young woman wrapped in my flannel on the bench seat of my rig.

She was so beautifully strange. Her bright purple hair was spread out like a fan behind her head, and makeup was smeared all over her face. Her lush body had all the curves a man could ask for, and I caught myself wondering what it would be like to hold her.

But her obvious beauty aside, there was the matter of her partial shift. I couldn't tell what her animal was at first glance, which was unusual. She didn't smell like a predator species, but she didn't smell like any of the prey I'd encountered, either. The only clues were the tufts of grey fur on her arms and the impressive claws on one hand.

The heavy, coppery tang of blood hit my nose and disrupted my musings. The scent of her blood made me twitch, but the familiar routine of first aid overrode that primal instinct... at least for now.

Moving away from her, I searched for my trusty first aid bag. Patching people up had a certain predictability to it I liked. It grounded me. With all the confusing feelings this stranger was evoking in me, I desperately wished to be grounded.

Each time I carefully bandaged a bleeding cut or picked a piece of glass out of her hair, I felt the prickle of something warm and comforting in my chest. This felt... right. Uncomfortably right. *Pull it together, asshole. She's a woman in distress, nothing more.*

My time as an Army medic had prepared me for just about anything that came my way. One thing my superiors always appreciated about me was the ability to remain calm in a crisis. Yet treating the bumps and bruises on this woman made me nervous.

Despite my best efforts, her wounds continued to bleed and there was no sign of her shifter accelerated healing. Her injuries were significant enough that it should have kicked in well before now, but the more I patched her up, the more I realized it just... wasn't. *What are you, Little Bit?*

The lack of progress made my chest heavy with worry.

My bear was exceptionally restless, clawing to be let out and protect this strange woman. I couldn't remember a time when I had felt him react to another person this way. It was as if he was telling me she was important. Someone more than just a good samaritan project. *She mattered to us.*

"Just a little longer, buddy," I murmured as I sprinkle the healing crystal dust from my first aid kit on the largest of her wounds and watched as the skin healed a little. "We'll go for a nice long run when we get back home."

But my initial hope that this would be an easy fix was fast disappearing. The crystal dust had only made a slight difference to her injuries, and I swore softly under my breath. We were fast approaching the extent of the treatment I could administer on the side of the road. This girl needed to be seen by a skilled healer, and soon.

I carefully scooted her further onto the bench seat and placed a seat belt over her legs. It would have to do. I sent a quick prayer up to the Moon Goddess that the woman would understand why I had to take her away and not accuse me of kidnapping her or something.

A tingle of awareness jolted through me when she moaned and clutched onto my flannel for dear life, burying her nose in it.

I dug in the side compartment and found the emergency green crystal that Asha and Glenda had practically forced me to add to my go-kit. They had insisted I carry it because it was imbued with the magic that, if deployed in time, could save virtually any supernatural life. I muttered a thanks for their foresight, and hung it on the door handle opposite her in the cab, and hoped for the best.

If this worked, I would buy the two of them the biggest cake in the whole damn town or anything else they wanted.

This woman was a stranger to me, yet the idea of her

dying or being hurt was so abhorrent that I felt physically ill at the mere idea.

It's time for a vacation. I am officially losing my shit.

The crystal glowed and illuminated the interior of my rig with an eerie green light. The woman cried out once, a sharp desperate cry of someone in pain… then she fell silent. Her breathing evened out and I finally exhaled.

"I'm gonna take care of you, Little Bit," I vowed to her. It made my bear happy to tell her that, even if she couldn't hear me.

Outside, the wreck was still blazing on the side of the road. I stomped at the embers with my heavy work boots and sprayed down the little patches of brush fire with my fire extinguisher. We got lucky. Her car was already a piece of shit, and it clearly didn't have a full tank of gas.

My bear took issue with her being so far away from the city so unprepared. Multiple terrible scenarios ran through my mind of people taking advantage of her while she was so isolated and alone. *People like… well… me.*

"Fuck, I am losing it." I muttered.

Satisfied that the fire was under control and not going to start a brush fire, I pawed through the debris to look for any personal effects that might give me a clue as to her identity.

Hidden under the smoldering door handle of the passenger side, a silvery object caught my eye. Hissing at the hot metal, I pulled a battered purse out of the wreckage. Flipping open the flap, the initials K.M . were stitched on the inside. A bright pink wallet and assortment of cosmetics and some old receipts were all resting on top of the jumbled mess. *Perfect.*

I reached for the wallet but stopped before opening it.

The thought of going through her things while she lay

unconscious and injured in my truck felt intrusive and wrong.

Clutching the scrap of silver to my chest, I finished spraying the rest of the wreck and grabbed the license plates off the burnt husk of a car.

This close to the vehicle, a myriad of scents assaulted my nose. Blood, gasoline, smoke and... something else. A light, almost floral scent. Eucalyptus with just a hint of rosemary. It filled my nose and settled down into my chest where something clicked into place.

MATE.

The feeling of certainty made me stumble backwards.

Oh. No. No, No, No. This isn't happening.

I looked back at my rig in a mixture of fascination and horror.

Every shifter dreamed of finding their mate someday. But when it hadn't happened by the time I turned 40, I figured Fate had different plans for me.

At 45, I'd grown comfortable with my solitary lifestyle. I came and went as I pleased, answering to no one. It was familiar. Controllable. Safe.

My bear wouldn't let me finish that train of thought. He pushed at my self-control so hard that I fell to my knees in my effort to prevent shifting.

She. Is. Our. Mate.

I lifted my face to the moon, the clear starry night above me, and roared. The sound echoed in the empty desert and a wild sense of protectiveness fell over me.

She was young and vibrant. I doubted she wanted an older bear stuck in his ways like me for a mate. For all I knew, she already had a mate and I would just be an annoyance in her otherwise perfect life.

If I'd learned anything in this brutal life, it was to set

your expectations low and early. That way you weren't disappointed.

Mate or not, I had a duty to this woman. I would protect her, make sure she was safe, and bring her to the healer.

Nothing more, nothing less. If I didn't get attached right away, her leaving wouldn't break me.

Grabbing her belongings, I stalked back to the rig and threw everything on the passenger seat. With exquisite carefulness, I put the truck in drive and headed down the highway going west.

It was time to go home to Misty Cove. Every few minutes, I checked in the mirror to see the faint outline of the woman lying on the bench, the green crystal glow illuminating her pale features.

I gripped the steering wheel tighter and punched the accelerator. Losing her wasn't an option. I picked up my cell phone and scrolled to the Oak Tree Coven entry and hit the dial button.

"Asha? It's Frank. I don't have a lot of time, I'm driving. Listen, I had to deploy the crystal. The woman is in my truck and we're on our way. We'll be there before lunch. Save her, Asha. You have to."

I hung up before Asha could ask me more questions and concentrated on driving. The soothing melodies of Taylor Swift piped out of my radio and I let myself fall into the rhythm of the road.

My bear settled down, content to keep watch over our mate while I kept watch on the road ahead. I was thankful for his curiosity and focus. If he hadn't paid such close attention to the little car that had been careening all over the road ahead of us, we might have missed finding our mate completely, or worse, run her down and killed her.

I shuddered at the thought. I didn't even know her

name, but the idea of being separated from her made my entire body hurt. It was powerful and disconcerting. We didn't even have a formalized matesbond and yet; I was inexplicably drawn to her.

My mate. My poor, injured mate who was being held together with magic and my attempts at first aid. Whatever happened, this... this was going to be a shitshow. I could feel it in my bones.

Chapter Five
Kalena

W as I dead? Or close to dead?

That would explain the pain. I had to be dead. Except, if I were dead — I was clearly in Hell because someone was being very loud, very close to my head. My head... my poor, throbbing head.

"She was partially shifted, bloody, and delirious. What was I supposed to do? Leave her for the fucking humans to have as a science experiment? I couldn't do that. No shifter deserves that. Besides, my bear... he... demanded I save her. I'm drawn to her... almost like a mate. Besides! If there was a time limit on that crystal, you should have damn well written it on there, dontcha think?" The angry voice yelled, his deep voice bouncing off the room and echoing around in my skull.

It made me groan. *Shut up. Shut up. Shut up.*

"Francis, you settle down *right now*. We are not your enemy. We are trying to help the poor woman. You can either speak to us calmly, or you can get out and let us work. What's it going to be?" This person much calmer. Her voice was authoritative and kind, but had enough of an edge that I definitely wouldn't cross her. Nope.

"My apologies, ma'am. I'm keyed up and my bear is worried."

My curiosity was getting the better of me and I concentrated on prying my eyes open while the conversation continued around me. *Was it absolutely necessary that they be this loud?*

"What kind of animal does she have? Do you know? Can you tell? She's not responding to treatment quickly. It could help the healing process if we had an idea." A third voice joined in, and this one sounded no-nonsense. *Oh goodie, more to the party.*

"How the fuck should I know, Glenda? She has some claws on her, grey fur, maybe an opossum? She doesn't smell like pred to me. I would know."

Whoever Mr. Gruff and Grumpy was, he was mad. I'd be mad, too if my name were Francis.

The name Francis triggered something in the back of my mind and I struggled to place it.

"Are you an opossum, I wonder?" someone asked very close to my ear.

Well. Offensive. Obviously, I am NOT an opossum. The nerve.

A clawing sensation in my chest startled me. My body had a visceral reaction to the word opossum.

Bright lights danced behind my eyes, and I forced them to open.

Which was, in hindsight, a mistake.

Everything was bright. Horrifically bright. *Blindingly bright.* It was so bright it took my breath away. *Nope. Do not want.*

I slammed my eyes shut immediately and tried to focus on my breathing.

"I will try her on the opossum formula, then."

The clawing sensation came back with a vengeance and forced me to pay attention. I felt personally offended by the word opossum, but I wasn't sure why.

"What, are you just guessing now? Is that even *safe?*" Mr. Gruff and Grumpy was back at it, at top volume. *Oh, Francis. Francis, Francis, Francis —*

"LIGHTEN UP, FRANCIS!" I yelled, opening my eyes wide and feeling triumphant. I had remembered! That felt like an accomplishment.

All noise in the room stopped immediately. For one blissful, single second there was complete silence. I looked around with interest, squinting to make out the figures that surrounded me.

When my eyes locked on to the only man in the group, I felt a strange jolt in my stomach. *Hello, Mr. Gruff and Grumpy.*

He was big. A tall, barrel-chested man in a faded flannel and worn jeans that fit like a glove. I realized after an awkward minute that I was staring at him, complete with mouth open and drool pooling in the corner of my mouth. *Lovely.*

Yet I couldn't look away. He drew me in with his rugged good looks, his beautiful brown eyes and the shock of dark hair peeking out under his ball cap. *A true mountain man.*

An older woman, her silver grey hair elegantly pulled back in a tasteful braid, stood on the other side of my bed. The other one looked barely older enough to drive. She was tiny, with bright pink pixie hair.

A snuffling sort of noise sounded from the one with the pink hair. At first, it started as a giggle masquerading as a cough, but soon it was a full-blown raucous laugh.

The older woman joined in and they cackled, leaning

on the bed to hold themselves up as they wiped tears from their eyes.

"Lighten... up... Francis..." one of them wheezed.

I was so confused. When I looked up at the man in question, he had a pained expression on his face, but he said nothing.

"What's so funny?" I asked. My mouth felt bone dry, and I looked around desperately for something to drink.

My question just cued off another round of laughter, and I leaned back on my pillow. My body was very reluctant to move and my limbs felt like giant weights anchoring me to the earth.

Maybe this was a dream. Or a hallucination. Or I'm dead.

A strangely familiar sensation swirled under my skin and distracted me from the recollection of pain. Eagerly, I latched onto it.

On instinct I balled that energy up and sent it zooming towards my frozen limbs, willing it to let me move again. The energy was pliable and responsive, and I felt in control, if only for a moment.

A warm, comforting feeling started in my fingers and toes and then raced up my veins, crashing into my chest like a powerful rubber band snap.

"ARGH!" I yelled out, flinging my arms and legs out like a deranged starfish.

"Moon *Fucking* Goddess!" Francis yelled, startled.

This time, my eyes opened easily. I looked around with interest, still squinting from the bright light. My arms and legs felt stiff and I tried to bring the energy ball back a little to relax them.

I went from being stiff as a board to feeling like a blob in under a second. *Might need to work on our energy skills.*

I didn't recognize where I was, but then again, not a lot made sense.

A bright exam light was shining directly over my head and a collection of candles and incense burned next to me on a skinny, metal table. The bed below me was extremely comfortable.

The entire room smelled strongly of basil, mint and pine.

"My name is Glenda, my dear. I am part of the Misty Cove Healing Arts Collective. Frank here," The older woman pointed at Mr. Gruff and Grumpy, "*Frank* rescued you from a terrible car accident in Nevada and brought you here to Misty Cove and over there is Asha, she's the witch in charge of your treatment." *Frank. Not Francis. Frank. Got it.*

"Hiya." Asha said, waving at me before looking down at the clipboard and scribbling some notes. She was holding a strange sort of crystal and I felt an urge, deep inside me, to stay away.

Frank-not-Francis cracked a half smile at me.

"Hi. Hi Frank and Glenda and Asha," I answered automatically.

My mouth was suddenly drier than sandpaper. I offered my hand, but when I looked at it, it was a deformed claw. I screamed, and they all took a step back.

"Oh my goddess, what is that?" I cried out, pulling back to look at it in abject horror.

My arms had both skin and fur, and my one hand was clearly a claw. *Fuck a wooden duck. Is that supposed to be like that? Have I always had a claw?*

"Do you know your name, dear?" My eyes flicked to Glenda.

I blinked. *Name. I had a name. I was sure of it. I just couldn't remember what it was.*

"Um, my brain is super foggy. I can't remember," I

finally said, my cheeks reddened with embarrassment. *What kind of person doesn't know their own name?*

Glenda traded glances with Asha and they both moved closer to me.

"Do you know your animal?" Asha asked abruptly, motioning with her pencil towards my claw hand. "Is it an opossum?"

"Nope." I said decisively.

"No, you don't know your animal, or no you aren't an opossum?" Asha pressed.

I thought about that. I wasn't honestly sure about much right now. My brain hurt and so did my body. But I was sure, in my heart of hearts, that I was 100% not an opossum.

"Not an opossum."

Asha looked annoyed at her theory being disproved, and I had a strange desire to stick my tongue out at her.

"Did you find anything that could identify her in the wreckage, Frank?" she asked, tiredly.

"Just her purse and her license plates. Her purse says K.M. on it."

"We're going to go through your bag, dear. Try to find out who you are!" Glenda announced, patting my hand gently.

I inclined my head in consent. Knowing who I was would make this entire process easier. I hoped they would tell me, too, once they found out. Fog swirled in my mind as I tried to recall... anything. There was a giant blank spot in my memory of how I got here.

Was I drugged? Am I going to be sold to some sort of crazy cartel? Is this where I die? Am I going to be locked up to be a breeder for some sort of crazed cult? I had so many questions.

Glenda interrupted my pity party, table of 1, with a barrage of questions I didn't know how to answer.

"Well, it looks like we have a ticket addressed to a K.M., a badge that says "I got lucky at Lucky Charmz," a tube of chapstick, a wallet with only cash in it, and what looks like a protection crystal. That's interesting. Crystals like this are typically only carried by magic users. It would be very unusual for a shifter to have the level of magic needed to use this. We'll have to do some tests. Maybe you use it for other reasons? Can you remember?"

I tried. I tried really, really hard. I *wanted* to come up with memories. They sounded pretty rad: *Lucky Charmz Club? Crystals? Magic Users? Shifters? That's the shit people should remember.*

Alas, I shook my head slowly. I had no recollection of that. The last thing I remembered was... Pain. Lots and lots of pain.

A word hovered on the tip of my tongue and I knew in my heart that it was important for them to know.

"Koaaa," I croaked. I wasn't even sure what that meant, but I felt satisfied that I said it. The clawing sensation in my chest stopped, and I was pleased.

"Ah, thank you, dear. That's most helpful." Glenda patted me again. Conversation all around me continued as if I didn't exist. Or maybe because I did? I couldn't tell.

Rude.

Asha fiddled with the crystal and muttered an incantation over it. Nothing happened at first. Then everything exploded in sound. It was so loud I wanted to clap my hands over my ears in protest, but when I tried, my hands felt frozen.

This was really, really annoying.

"We don't mean to be intrusive, dear, although it must feel that way," Glenda started, soothingly.

"We just wanted to confirm your status so we can make sure the healing potion is correct for both your natures. In

46

order for you to heal properly, we need to use magic that is compatible with your shifter side. That's all. We are all very concerned for your health and safety and only want to double-check all potions," Asha continued.

Oh. Well. Now I feel like a complete asshole.

"Oh," I mumbled awkwardly, "I'm sorry. Everything is jumbled. I know what I am, I just can't seem to *say* it."

Glenda regarded me. "Close your eyes and take a breath. Try to connect with your animal. Perhaps she is frightened from the car accident."

I stared at her blankly. *What the what now? Is this even real?*

I glanced up at Frank in a panic and pinched myself.

"How long have I been out? What day is it? What happened?"

Before he could answer, my blood pressure shot up and I felt my skin prickling again.

A sense of foreboding shot through me. I knew what this was. I didn't know my name, how I got here, or what day it was… but this I knew.

"Oh no," I moaned miserably, "I don't think I can stop it."

"Stop what? What's happening? Asha." Frank leaned over me with concern etched across his face.

I wanted to cry. I couldn't remember my birthday, or what I did last week but *this. This I remembered.*

My body contorted in painful spasms and I gasped in short, shallow breaths, throwing myself back against the pillow. The tufts of hair on my arms grew and more popped out on my neck and my legs. A searing pain sprang from my scalp and I cried out, writhing on the bed while the three strangers looked on helplessly.

"Oh my," Glenda said, peering down at me in concern. "Is it like that every time?"

I shrugged. "I think so. I can't really remember much.

47

My brain feels foggy and everything prior to just now is lurking in the fog, just out of reach."

The clawing sensation in my chest demanded attention, and the word popped into my mind. *Koala.*

"Koala," I said miserably. I pulled the sheet over my fur covered arms and tried to burrow into the covers further and hide. "I think that's what I am. A mutant koala."

Glenda and Asha traded a long look that made me very nervous.

"I think I understand the crystal now," Asha said triumphantly, pulling out a measuring tape to measure the little ears that had popped up on my head. *Gods this is humiliating.*

Frank was staring at me with an inscrutable expression of longing on his face, and I wanted to die from the embarrassment.

Asha and Glenda both reassured me that all was well and got up to retrieve whatever they needed to heal me, leaving me alone with Frank and my fuzzy fucking arms... and awkward silence.

Chapter Six
Kalena

"Soooo" I looked at him and then back down at my claw. *Ugh. There's a chance this is still just... a really intense dream. Or a hallucination. Or... yeah. Something.*

Glenda had left me a bottle of water on the table, and it was just out of reach. Frank saw me reaching and hurried over to hand it to me.

"Do you need help? This is called water. Do you know it?"

I stared at him. *Is he crazy, too?*

"Uh, I think I got it, big guy. Thanks…"

He handed me the bottle and looked back down at the floor. His ruddy cheeks were tinted pink in embarrassment.

"Sorry. When you said your memory was gone, I wasn't sure how far that went."

I tried not to laugh but his earnestness was just... So endearing. The man legitimately thought I had forgotten how to drink water and he was ready to jump in and save the day. A part of me wished I would have let him. Something about being hand-fed by this rugged Adonis was very, very appealing.

"Yeah. I can't remember how I got here or, you know,

my name but... I haven't forgotten how to exist. At least I don't think so. I feel like I understand the basics. I can comprehend the conversation we are having. I know I like mangos, but not strawberries. I prefer Earl Grey tea over coffee. I know the pain I feel is because my shifting is wrong. I can't remember why it's wrong, though."

I also know I have a thing for men with thick beards and thicker thighs that I can ride for days... Stop that.

He gave that some thought and nodded heavily, rubbing his eyes and yawning.

We sat in awkward silence for a few minutes, each lost in our own thoughts. His presence was making me increasingly aware of a dull ache in my core that had nothing to do with recovering from an accident and everything to do with... him. *He smells like pine, but I wonder what he tastes like?*

I was officially losing my mind and possibly jumping off the deep end of the horny pool at this point and I couldn't be bothered to care.

"Are you a shifter, too?" I asked finally. Curiosity about him burned through me.

He exhaled slowly and lifted those deep brown eyes to mine. *Soulful eyes.*

"Yes. *Ursus arctos californicus* otherwise known as the California Grizzly," he tapped his fingers against his jean-covered thigh.

Californicus? More like Californicate— what is WRONG with me?! Was I always this... extra?

He fell silent again for a long while, and I felt anxious. I don't know why I needed him to accept me, but it was suddenly extremely important to me.

"I brought your purse from the wreck. It doesn't have ID in it. But it has initials. K.M." Frank offered and I nodded pensively.

K.M. didn't ring a bell at all. *Shit.*

I stretched out on the bed and snuggled deeper into the flannel that was draped over my shoulders. It smelled utterly divine, and I inhaled deeply before I let out a contented little sigh. If I had to be stuck in a room with the sexiest man I ever remembered meeting as a half human, half koala hybrid with limited memories… this was as good as it was probably going to get. *Slow clap, brain. Slow freaking clap.*

Frank stood suddenly and started pacing, his eyes wild and nervous.

"You ok, buddy?" I asked, eyeing him curiously. He didn't answer, and I shrugged and tried to make myself comfortable. Contrary to popular belief, morphing only half your body into an animal was not half-as-painful. Or at least, I didn't think it was. I couldn't remember what it felt like to fully shift.

Something round and hard in my pocket kept catching on the sheets. I held up my claw hands and looked down at my body and shuddered.

Nope. That's not gonna fly.

"Uh, Frank?" I asked, bravely.

He turned to face me immediately, and the intense look on his rugged face took my breath away.

"Yes?" His deep gravelly voice washed over me like a soothing balm, and I shivered. *Fuck, I am all over the place today.*

"I need your help," I squirmed on the bed and bit my lip in mortification.

"There's something in my pocket. My front pocket. Can you -" I inhaled sharply and dropped my gaze to the floor, "Can you please help me get it out? I can't. My claws."

He was silent for a beat before he moved over to me and his hands hovered over the sheet. The overwhelming scent of a pine forest after a rainstorm surrounded me and made every nerve ending in my body wake up and scream for attention.

Quickly and efficiently, he peeled the sheet away from my body and reached over to the pocket I pointed at with my claw.

With one large hand anchoring my hip, he slid two fingers into the tight pocket of my jean shorts and fished out a brassy-looking coin and handed it to me.

My skin reacted immediately under his gentle touch. A slow-moving fire spread out from my hip and down my limbs, making me bite my lip to keep from moaning. My heart was hammering against my chest. I was drawn to him like a magnet and it threatened to overwhelm me.

When he straightened and removed his hands, pulling the sheet back over me and tucking me in gently, I felt a profound sense of loss.

"It's official. I'm turning into a nutcase," I whispered under my breath before looking at the coin that he had placed on the sheet next to me. I tapped it with my claw and tried to remember its significance.

The coin glowed the more I played with it, and the words along the side became brighter. It wasn't a language I was familiar with. Frank stared at it and then back at me and then abruptly left the room. *Awkward. Ok.*

"WE'RE BACK!" Glenda sang out, pushing a trolley cart with an assortment of beakers on it. Asha followed her, carrying a large crystal and what looked like a bag of dirt.

"Oh, what's that you've got there?" Glenda asked, peering at my coin with interest.

"It's nothing," I stammered.

But Glenda wasn't paying attention. Her eyes were locked on the coin and her hands were shaking.

"My dear. Would you mind terribly if I looked at that coin for just a moment? I won't steal it or anything like that, I just want to read it."

I hesitated for a long moment. The longer the coin was in my possession, the more attached I felt to it. Curiosity about the inscription won out, and I handed it over.

Glenda received it reverently and held it up to the light. Asha came over to look at it and she too looked amazed.

"Where did you get this?" she breathed, reaching out with a finger to touch the edge lightly.

"I... found it. In my pocket." I mumbled.

"Do you know what this is, child?" Glenda asked, placing the coin back in my palm, "When did it start glowing?"

I looked down at it again and shrugged. I couldn't even tell them my name, much less answer questions about weird pocket coins. *#priorities*

"Right, while Glenda sorts out your golden mystery there. Let's you and I sort out your shifter, eh?" Asha dumped the dirt on the ground and spread it out, making a salt circle around it and then planting the crystal in the middle.

Once the dirt had been arranged to her satisfaction, she stepped over the salt circle and brought forth a ball of bright red pulsing energy. I jumped back and squeaked at her. This was all getting too weird and I wanted to leave. Preferably now.

Panic filled me and I edged closer and closer towards the end of the exam table and eyed the door longingly.

Out in the hallway, I heard raised voices, and I craned my neck towards the door in alarm. When the door burst open, I leapt back in terror and both Glenda and Asha whirled around. Glenda had partially shifted her hands to fearsome claws and Asha looked like she was ready to hex the intruder into the next plane. It was both badass and completely terrifying. *Memo to self: do not piss off Asha OR Glenda.*

Frank looked up at the sound of my screech and froze, causing a smaller, blonder man to crash into him. Where Frank was tall and barrel-chested and exuded a sense of wild power, the man with him was best described as compact. He was short but fit, with a lean physique and white-blonde hair. He exuded kindness and something else, something that called to me in a similar way that Frank did. They both intrigued me, and I could feel that strange sense of power under my skin again.

Asha glared at Frank before going back to her dirt and chanting, releasing the red energy directly into the crystal in the dirt and observing it as it turned bright blue.

Asha stepped out of the circle and picked up the crystal that was glowing a deep teal color and handed it to me, maneuvering me to stand in the dirt pile.

Pressing her thumb on my forehead, she muttered an incantation, and I felt energy rushing up from the ground and flowing through my legs and core. When it reached my heart, it stopped and I coughed heavily.

Asha opened her eyes and looked at me with satisfaction.

"Huh. Just as I suspected. You aren't *just* a koala. You are part witch and you have a block on your magic. A powerful one. But," she chuckled, "Not as powerful as me." She took the crystal back and examined it.

"Yeah, see, this crystal represents your earthen body. When we heal it with the earth energy, it flows up from bottom to top. The energy of Gaia flows through us and heals through our chakras. Your energy flows fine from root, sacral and solar plexus but it is blocked at your heart level." Asha pointed out the strange yellow spot that had appeared midway on the crystal.

I nodded as if I understood and then went back to staring at Frank and the new guy. I thought Frank embodied the perfect male specimen, but when I saw the guy next to him, I had strange butterflies in my stomach again. *Oh God, maybe the accident knocked out my filter and I am just a sex fiend who is about to be set loose on this poor city. Like… a deranged koala succubus or something.*

The new guy was definitely watching me back with interest and I preened under the attention. *What? If two hot men want to look at me like I'm candy when I'm a fuzzy freak, I'm gonna go with it!*

Asha shoved me back towards the bed and then returned to her circle, muttering something and shaking the crystal. I stopped paying attention to her. My brain was tired and when presented with magic I didn't understand vs two exhibits of delicious mancandy to stare at, mancandy always wins.

Something about them called to me. Maybe it was just lust and the novelty of having both of their attention on me at the same time. But it felt deeper. It was strange and powerful all at once. Almost as if an invisible tether was reaching out from my heart and connecting to each one of them. *If this is a nervous breakdown, it's more fun than they show on TV.*

The feeling seemed mutual, at least for the new guy. He was staring at me as if I'd hung the moon myself. Frank was glowering at me, but in a grumpy, protective way.

It made me feel all warm and sunshiney inside.

I am going to need serious help once I figure out what is going on here. And therapy. And maybe a couple potions. Or wine.

"What's your name?" I asked, nodding towards New Guy.

"It's Chuck," he answered quickly.

Frank and Chuck. Solid names. You can't go wrong with Frank. Or Chuck. Sure wish I knew what *my* name was. *If I never remember, do I get to pick a new one? What name would I choose? Maybe Frank and Chuck could name me... after they finished making me co.....*

The intensity of my thoughts freaked me out, and I cleared my throat awkwardly. My cheeks felt hot and I hoped they didn't notice.

Tapping the weird coin again, I stared up at the ceiling and wished I could remember literally *anything* about my life before I woke up in Misty Cove. But it was all a giant blank. *Ugh.*

A strange shimmer started in the corner of the room, followed by blinding rays of rainbow light. I threw my hand up to shield my eyes and heard the deep roar of a pissed off bear and the hiss of an angry cat bounce throughout the room.

When the light subsided, I gingerly opened my eyes and blinked.

A copper-haired, bare-chested man in bright green booty shorts stood at the foot of my bed.

"Do you see him too?" I half-whispered to Frank, unable to take my eyes off this glittery apparition.

Frank didn't answer and I dragged my eyes away from Glittery McSmexy to look at him.

Frank was gone. A giant brown Grizzly bear was in the corner, standing on his hind legs and growling. *Oh my, Smokey. What big... paws you have.*

Asha was standing just out of Frank's reach with an angry-looking ball of red light in her palm and a gorgeous lynx crouched next to her. Chuck hadn't transformed into anything but he held a wicked-looking knife and a calm look of readiness that told me he absolutely knew how to use his weapon.

The protectiveness of my new friends was oddly touching.

My golden visitor shimmered and crossed his arms across his chest.

"Are you an angel? Am I dead? Are you taking me to the afterlife?" I asked quietly.

The golden man blinked, and concern marred his perfect face.

"Kalena, lass, are you high?" he asked bluntly.

"You know my name? My name is Kalena?" I asked excitedly. *Golden boy wasn't just a pretty face, he had information!*

"What do you mean, is your name Kalena? Of course it is? What happened to you?" he asked, moving to the side of the bed and reaching out to grab my hand.

Glitter fell all over the bedspread and Frank growled fiercely. The sparkly man looked around and sighed.

Kalena. My name is Kalena. It's a pretty name. I like it. It... suits me. Kalena the Koala? My parents must have had a sense of humor.

"What else do you know about me? Who are you?" I asked eagerly.

He swore viciously in a language I didn't recognize and turned to face the rest of the room.

"And what did you do to her, eh? Did you steal the Anam Cara from her? Hex her so she would give it to you? If you hurt her, you will not leave this room alive." he roared. Golden light sprang from his fingertips and I gasped aloud. *Whoa. Talk about protective instincts.*

I knew I should have been scared or, at the very least, horrified. But I wasn't. I was turned on and drawn to the golden stranger just as strongly as I had reacted to Frank and Chuck.

"Who the fuck are you?" Chuck asked with a deadly edge to his calm voice.

"Belfast," the stranger snapped back. *Belfast. That's a weird name. But it suits him.*

"Right, *Belfast*, and what do you want with her?" Chuck continued, stepping forward with his knife at the ready.

"I came to rescue her, Sea World. And clearly not a moment too soon."

The shiny golden man looked at me aghast and took a step forward, eliciting a fearsome growl from Frank-the-bear.

"Ah, shut it, Pooh Bear," he snapped before turning back to me, "*A stór,* what happened to you? Do you remember me? Belfast?"

I stared at him hard, willing myself to remember. It felt criminal to not remember a man this deliciously hot.

But my mind was blank. I had zero recollection of anyone named Belfast.

Slowly, I shook my head and he looked…. crushed.

"Um, are we… involved?" I squeaked, mortified again. Frank snarled from his corner and my eyes widened.

Belfast chuckled and pinched the bridge of his nose, dislodging a fine mist of golden glitter off his arm.

"No, *a stór,* I cannot lie to you. We were not involved but… I had hoped to change that."

Frank growled again and then shifted smoothly into his human form. My eyes nearly bugged out of my head when he moved to stand next to Belfast bare-ass naked.

Frank towered over the golden man but they both had impressive muscles. I stared at them without speaking for another moment, my eyes flicking between Belfast, Frank and Chuck.

A feeling like a rubber band snap hit my chest and I fell backwards onto the pillow.

"Mine." I whispered before my eyes rolled back in my head.

Chapter Seven
Chuck

When Frank dragged me here to the clinic to see the woman he had rescued off the side of the road, I thought he was crazy. But the moment I laid eyes on the strange woman in the hospital bed, her vibrant purple hair spreading out over the pillow like a halo, I was glad he did.

Mate.

The dolphin song rang true in my heart the moment I locked eyes on her, and a sense of peace washed over me. *I had a mate.*

She was beautiful.

Frank had clued me in that she was having trouble with her memories because of the accident. My heart ached for her and I wanted to make it all better.

She was sitting up in bed holding a glowing coin. A flash of realization blazed in my chest. This scene was familiar.

When my Sea Lion MC brothers found their mate, Ronnie, last summer, it was because she just waltzed into town with a glowing necklace that proved to be one of the mythical Matestones. *Could this really be happening again?*

Fate was playing games with us.

Somehow, Misty Cove had attracted yet another stranger with a Matestone. I was sure of it.

I didn't know what was so special about our little town, but at this moment, I was filled with gratitude to Fate for giving us this chance.

For years, our pods and packs had remained empty and my fellow shifters of all species had moved on—destined to search the Earth for the loves that Fate designated for them, but that few ever found.

Matestones had been out of circulation for so many years that I couldn't believe they even still existed. But that was before Ronnie showed up.

A supernatural chemistry-tracker, the Matestone was unique. It never forced mates to choose each other or bond, it just allowed a preview of the peace and love that came from a completed bond. The more compatible you were with a potential mate, the more peace and attraction you felt when a Matestone was involved.

Legend said Fate created them long ago to form packs and pods and covens that maximized the strength of different supes centered on the holder of the Matestone.

Our society was predominantly matriarchal, meaning the Matestone holder was usually female. It wasn't uncommon to have pods as large as five or six, all working in harmony to please their mate and live together as a family.

Family.

All I'd *ever* wanted was a family of my own.

A home filled with love and laughter.

My MC brothers had given me a family of sorts. They'd taken me in when no one else would. Hell, Trevor practically raised me when I washed ashore, but I'd always wanted more. I wanted to come home to my mate and the rest of her pod and build a life together as a unit.

Frank was clearly one of her mates and it looked as if the new guy, Belfast, was, too. When she claimed us in a word, my heart leapt for joy until she passed out from the shock.

Frank and Belfast were too busy posturing and arguing to notice what they were doing to her. *Our Kalena.*

I wanted to push past them and go to her, hold her tired, broken body in my arms and tell her that everything was going to be ok now. We found her. Her pod was here.

But I didn't.

Our mate was hurting. She needed time. She barely knew her own name, much less what a Matestone was. We owed her the opportunity to rest. To choose us properly, after we had wooed her and shown her the life she could have with us.

My MC brothers always said a potential mate was someone to be treasured, not fought over like rabid dogs. We were sophisticated, unlike the wolves.

Frank and Belfast's argument escalated into a shoving match. Frank pushed Belfast and a small cloud of glitter puffed out from his chest to sprinkle the floor.

Kalena's sharp intake of breath spurred me to action.

"Hey, guys?" I called out quietly, "Guys, she needs to rest."

They didn't listen, and I let out a huff of exasperation. Being underestimated wasn't new to me. People and fellow supes had underestimated me my entire life. Trevor told me once it was because I blended in too much. *Whatever that meant.*

True, I'd never been the huge muscle-bound enforcer type like Frank, all growls and intimidating postures. I'd also never been the pretty one, dazzling others with my beauty like Belfast-the-glitterbomb seemed to be.

All my life, I'd been the one that existed in the background. A run-of-the-mill motorcycle mechanic. Neither tall nor short, not skinny, but not jacked either. I was solidly *medium* in everything.

Add in my light blonde hair, baby blue eyes and the eternal babyface that all dolphins were cursed with and Trevor was right. No matter how many years I racked up, the guys at the Clubhouse still referred to me as The Kid, and I really *did* just blend into the background.

I turned my attention back to the argument and raised my eyebrows in concern at the way the blood seemed to drain from Kalena's face. She looked deathly pale and worried.

This had to stop.

Belfast raised his voice to Frank and Kalena bit her lip, her eyes dancing between the two of them.

Wedging myself between Frank and Belfast, I put a palm on each of their chests and pushed outward.

"Get out of the way, Chuck," Frank growled.

I stood my ground, pushing my hands harder into their respective chests and forcing them apart. My strength wasn't as noticeable as Frank's but throwing around motorcycles every day was not for the feeble.

"You're upsetting Kalena with your bullshit posturing. That's not how pods work!" I gritted out. Frank leaned into my hand, forcing me to back up a few steps.

"Who said anything about a pod? What the fuck is a *pod?*" Belfast smirked, batting my hand away as if it were nothing.

I looked helplessly at Kalena and noted how avidly she was watching us.

"Walk. It. Off." I shoved as hard as I could at Frank and Belfast. My dolphin was worked up, and I allowed him to lead the way.

When we were swimming in the ocean, my dolphin

could tune into the electrical currents of fish and find them that way. It was a strange sort of perk that only Guiana Dolphins had. A sort of buzzy electro-location. In my human form, that ability had more applicable uses - I could harness the electrical current of any living form and briefly hold it before slamming it back into them.

Basically, my dolphin allowed me to be a human taser.

As soon as the charge slammed back into Frank and Belfast, they sprang apart and shook their hands out while the current ran through them. Frank's eyes turned yellow and he bared his teeth at me. Belfast just looked shocked and slightly…. impressed.

"The fuck was that, eh?" Belfast brushed more glitter off his chest before crossing his arms and glaring at me. I stepped towards him, determined to give him a piece of my mind but before I could get it out his eyes widened and he stared over my shoulder.

"Uh, you might want to move, little shockwave!" he warned, pointing and stepping back.

I partially turned, but I was too slow. Frank in all his rage-filled glory was towering over me with his arm cocked.

"You little shit!" Frank growled before his fist plowed into my face. The crisp wet sound of an impact and the subsequent rush of blood down my face told me that my nose was actually broken.

Kalena let out an ear-splitting shriek that grabbed all of our attention.

"Are you out of your goddamn minds?!!" she yelled, pointing at me with a horrified expression on her face.

"He was here for *me*, not you. How dare you!"

Frank and Belfast looked at the floor sheepishly.

"Are you done with the pissing contest?" she asked them icily.

They both managed a tight nod, and she rolled her eyes before beckoning me to come closer and sit on the bed next to her. Glenda peeked in and clucked disapprovingly at the four of us before leaving, hopefully she'd bring back an ice pack and a stiff drink. My shifter nature allowed me to heal quickly but the extra attention was definitely welcome.

When Glenda returned, she made eye contact with all of us and I let out a sigh of relief to see the ice pack in her hand.

"I want to know more about this," she started, holding up the golden coin. It was glowing a faint blueish color, I was mesmerized by it.

"Where do you want to begin, dear?" Glenda asked, looking at Asha for support as she pressed the ice pack to my face.

"I want to know everything," Kalena leaned forward and propped herself up against the wall for support. "But especially why I feel possessive and needy around these three asshats."

Frank, Belfast, and I all looked at each other uneasily. As far as first-time-pod-meeting, this was not going well.

"Should I go get Ronnie?" I finally asked quietly, looking to Glenda and Asha for clarification. They nodded, and I quietly left the room to track down the one person in this town who could probably explain this better than anyone else.

BY THE TIME I reached Buoy 6 Bar & Cafe, I was pretty worked up.

The way Kalena had looked at all of us with a mixture of revulsion and horror was like a harpoon straight to my heart. *What if she hates us? What if we ruined our one chance of bonding with her? What if I ruined it?*

The parking lot was full of cars and motorcycles, lots and lots of motorcycles, and I cursed under my breath. The likelihood of keeping the existence of a second Matestone under wraps just decreased dramatically. Taking a deep breath, I pushed my way through the swinging doors and stepped into the blessed air conditioning.

A loud group of men in matching leather jackets were gathered around the counter. They were hard at work teasing a woman wearing an apron that said "Sealions Do It Better." I watched as they each took turns grabbing her and kissing the crap out of her. The Sea Lion MC pod worshipped their mate, and another wave of jealousy went through me.

I wanted that. I wanted my pod more than anything else in the world.

"Ronnie!" I called out, making my way through the scrum of people to reach her.

She turned her smiling face on me and leaned over the counter to kiss my cheek in greeting.

"What's up, Chuck?" she cackled merrily and snapped her dishtowel at Earl who was busy trying to cop a feel.

"Um, we need you at the clinic," I started quietly, looking around to minimize eavesdropping.

Bryan and Trevor both sat up and leaned forward. "The clinic? What's going on, Chuck?"

I stared at my feet and took a deep breath.

"I think I found my mate. It's… I just need you to come to the clinic, please?" I asked her quietly.

Ronnie studied my face for a minute and then looked down at the two rings she wore stacked on her right hand and twisted them. One was fairy gold that was luminous and the palest gold color, the other was a deep onyx black.

"Kalena?" she asked. The men around her inhaled sharply before turning en masse to stare at me.

"How did you know?" I asked, mystified.

"Uhh, long story. I got a heads up last year at the Surf Festival from the Fae. Let's go. I'll explain it all later."

Ronnie kissed all of her men goodbye and followed me out the door of the cafe back towards the clinic without another word.

Glenda and Asha both greeted her with warm hugs, and even Frank and Belfast gave her a cordial welcome. Ronnie has that kind of effect on people. Even if you didn't know that she was a Matestone Guardian, she had a personality that drew you in. You wanted to be around her.

Ronnie waited until we all assembled in chairs around Kalena's bed before she parked herself on an ottoman and started fishing around in her ample cleavage for a crystal pendant that was wrapped in silver thread.

She waved it at Kalena.

"Hi there, I'm Ronnie. Show you mine if you show me yours?"

I forced a laugh at the absurdity of it all as Kalena grabbed her coin and held it up.

"Asha says she thinks it's the earth energy one," she offered. I turned questioningly to Asha, but she just shooed me and turned her attention back to Ronnie and Kalena. *Apparently a lot of conversation took place while I was away.*

Ronnie nodded and waved hers again, "Mine is water energy, for sure. I mean, my mates are a pod of freaking sea lions."

"You're human?!" Kalena asked in surprise after a moment.

Ronnie grinned, "Born and bred. But I've got some added stuff from the Fae and whatever-the-fuck Bill is." She pointed to two rings on her right hand. Kalena looked confused, but nodded agreeably. Her eyes kept drifting to Belfast's bare chest, and I had to tamp down the jealousy that sprouted there.

Ronnie folded her hands and leaned forward.

"So, let me guess. You've never heard of a Matestone and you just kind of happened upon it randomly? It was a gift, or you found it and then it started changing and suddenly you ended up here? Is that about right?"

Wide-eyed, Kalena nodded. "I think so? I don't have a lot of memory of how I got it. I just woke up here, actually."

Belfast raised his hand and stepped forward.

"It's Leprechaun-made. She pulled it out of my pot of gold last night in the parking lot of the Lucky Charmz Club where we both work. I meant to only give her some gold, but she chose the coin and I believe it's the *Anam Cara*."

Ronnie looked Belfast up and down, her eyes lingering momentarily on the emerald green booty shorts that hugged his sculpted hips.

Kalena scowled at her, and her blatant possessiveness gave me hope.

Ronnie smiled widely, "Do you mean to tell me you—" she pointed at Kalena, "went digging around in his pot of gold last night," she pointed back at Belfast and waggled her eyebrows, "and managed to grab a priceless Fae artifact that is also a Matestone?"

Kalena froze and then shrugged, her face a picture of uncertainty, "That's what they tell me."

Ronnie threw her head back and laughed so hard tears streamed from her eyes and smudged her mascara all over her face.

"Oh my god," she gasped, "I'm so glad you're here. You're my new favorite person."

Frank's grumpy growl brought her back to business. She stuck her tongue out at the formidable bear shifter and I had to smile.

Ronnie was a fucking delight and I meant that with total sincerity. Her outlook and joy for life was mesmerizing.

"What do you know about the Fae?" she asked Kalena kindly, "Do you have any memories about the Fae, remember anything about them?"

Belfast looked slightly paler than normal and he started fidgeting with a piece of gold, flipping it between his fingers as he tapped his foot on the floor.

"I think... Everything in me says stay out of Fae business unless asked to be part of it. Is that right?" Kalena hedged.

Ronnie toyed with a ring on her finger and nodded. "Pretty much. Ok, so, a representative of the Fae came by Misty Cove this past summer when the whole Matestone thing was happening with me and my guys. Basically, we're Guardians of the Matestones. Not just chosen to have a harem or something, but we were chosen for a *reason*. The Guardians haven't been called for a century. The Fae are really interested in this turn of events, not because they mean us harm, but because Fate is getting involved again. Dakira was the representative from the Summer Court and she told me to watch out for you. She said another one was coming, someone like me, and she knew your name."

The room was silent for a moment as Ronnie allowed Kalena to process that turn of events.

"Now, have you formed any attachments yet? Felt anything weird, like you're being drawn towards anyone in particular?" Ronnie finally asked Kalena.

The tension in the room rocketed up as Frank, Belfast and I all leaned forward to hear her answer.

She hesitated, and her face flushed. "Everything feels weird? I woke up here. Frank saved me. I found out I have a block on my magic and my koala is all a mess, and I don't have memories... I have *claws*. I don't know that I have had time to think about attachments. I just learned my name. But, there's something... I feel drawn to *them*. Possessive, almost. I don't know why."

Ronnie studied her seriously before looking back at the three of us.

"Boys," she warned. We all straightened up and tried not to pressure our mate. *She is ours. I know it.*

Ronnie nodded encouragingly, "Well, that's ok. You haven't really been around too many people yet and you have had a helluva day. I can only compare my experience, but you will definitely feel something when the Matestone is working for you. Pay attention to your emotions and remember, fated mates are tricky. You can reject a mate before the bond takes place and everything is cool, but if you enter a matesbond with someone, it's permanent. You can take as many mates as you feel connected to. Packs, pods, covens—it's always more than two."

"What if I want to stay single? Can I just, I don't know, give the Matestone to someone who wants to be mated?" she asked, unable to meet Ronnie's gaze.

Frank tensed, his fingers partially shifting enough to dig into the wooden armrest of the chair with a loud *crack*.

"Hey, look at me," Ronnie reached over the bedspread and grabbed Kalena's arm. "I know how hard it is to wrap your head around this bullshit. And you have it harder than me because you still need to heal and figure out what happened to you. Just know this: the timeline is, more or less, in your control. You have until the Matestone timer runs out to choose your mates and cement your mates-bonds. The rest of your relationship is for you and that person, or people, to negotiate. No one is going to force you into anything… as long as you choose."

Icy fear spiraled down my spine. I had forgotten the time constraints.

"And if I don't choose?" Kalena asked timidly.

Ronnie closed her eyes and pinched the bridge of her nose. "The Council will choose for you. There are rules that go with these Matestones. I would highly encourage you not to let that happen. The Council has good people on it, but not being able to choose sounds horrible to me."

"Fuck. That." Frank spat out, standing up and turning to pace the small office.

"You're meant for us. My bear knows it, Chuck knows it, and—and—whatever the fuck that one is, he knows it, too. You belong with *us*, not whoever the Council decides!" he growled at her.

"It's Leprechaun, fur ball," Belfast snapped. Frank growled again.

Kalena squirmed uneasily. Her cheeks were a pretty shade of bright red.

"You don't have to choose now," he continued pacing the length of the small room, "We—" he pointed to Belfast and me, "are going to woo you until you know what we know! We will do everything we can to help you get your memories back! I vow on my bear!"

Ronnie smirked at us and then winked at Glenda and Asha.

"My work here is done," she said with a smile. "Call me if you have questions, babe. I'm usually at Buoy 6 or at the Clubhouse. Come by anytime." She sashayed out of the office without another word.

Kalena examined her claws before she finally looked up at us. I wouldn't blame her if she turned tail and ran for her life after all of that.

"Ok."

My heart leaped in my chest and my dolphin wanted to sing out in joy.

"Ok?" I asked, stepping forward to place my hand on the bedspread.

"I want you to help me. I still don't know about any matesbonds or anything like that but... if you are offering help, I accept. From each of you."

Belfast, Frank and I exchanged glances and then looked back at our mate with smiles on our faces.

"Just to be clear, you are asking us to woo you? To show you how great it could be if we were matesbonded?" I asked, carefully.

Kalena looked thoughtful and then a shy smile spread across her face and she nodded.

"I'm... drawn to you guys and I don't know why. I guess I just want to explore that and see what happens. I've never felt like this before and it's exciting. Is that ok?"

We all spoke up, talking over each other in our haste to reassure her. It was more than ok. My dolphin knew she was our mate and the fact that she was consenting to our pursuit of her filled me with hope and anticipation.

Challenge accepted.

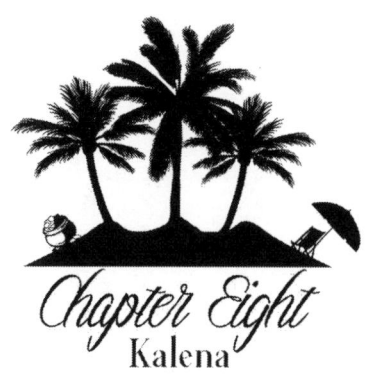

Chapter Eight
Kalena

After Ronnie, Frank, Belfast and Chuck all left, my energy levels bottomed out completely and all I wanted was a nap. Before I passed out, Glenda and Asha managed to get a tonic in me that forced my koala to allow me to fully shift back to human.

I barely had the energy to thank them before sleep hit me. When I awoke, the sun was streaming through the window and I was starving.

Asha had left a small flowery journal next to my bed with the events of the last day written out to help jog my memory.

"Kalena Montague. Lucky Charmz Club. Matestone. Frank. Belfast. Chuck. Mates." I read every word out loud, wracking my brain for more memories or anything that was strong enough to break through the fog. There was another entry with a new date and I read it twice to be sure.

Patient slept for 48 hours after administration of the tonic. Shift remained stable.

I slept for two entire days?! No wonder I felt hungry enough to eat a bear! My mind immediately went to the bear who had rescued me, and a different kind of hunger perked up. Frank was growly AF but he had a certain wild charm about him that, now that I wasn't bleeding and dazed on the side of the road, I could appreciate a little more. Those gigantic hands of his, the way he looked at me like I was something precious to cherish and protect?

Yeah. It worked for me. I was probably batshit crazy and for all I knew, this was a really complicated hallucination or dream. If that was the case, I wasn't in any hurry to wake up or return to everyday life.

Mostly healed, no longer furry, and refreshed—I tried to reflect on my situation with a rational mind.

I was in Misty Cove, California in some sort of supe healing clinic.

I had little-to-no memory of my life before I got here.

At some point I had acquired a Matestone and activated it. That part was a little fuzzy.

But because of that Matestone, three men were claiming they felt matebonds with me. Three handsome, vastly different, sexy men—who I had *literally just met*.

And to make matters worse? I felt something for them. Maybe it was Stockholm Syndrome, maybe it was delirium, but... I felt off without them next to me. There was a strange pull in my chest, like I was being gently tugged on from three different directions.

It wasn't painful, but it wasn't pleasant either.

"Ah, Kalena darling, you're awake! I bet you're half starved. Come, dear. We'll have breakfast with Asha in the sunroom. You need to get some fresh air." Glenda bustled into the room with a bright smile that made me feel like pure sunshine was shining directly into my soul.

Glenda may be the best part of Misty Cove. Followed closely by Belfast's ass, Frank's hands, and Chuck's soulful

74

eyes that pierced my heart. *Ugh, woman, eat something. You're getting sappy. It's gross.*

Someone had left a small blue backpack on the ottoman at the foot of the bed for me and I was overjoyed to see a couple changes of clothes, a small bag of cosmetics, and a toothbrush. Changing quickly into a simple tank top and shorts, I ran a brush through my tangled hair and threw it all up into a messy bun. A new shimmery grey streak ran through my hair and I scowled at it in the mirror. The grey stood out dramatically next to the vibrant purple and I was not pleased. *Memo to self: find a hairdresser. Stat.*

Following my nose, I meandered through the hallway of the small clinic and found myself in a sunny covered porch. Floor-to-ceiling bookshelves covered one complete wall, and they overflowed with a collection of colorful paperbacks and ancient looking tomes. The floor was a bright terracotta tile decorated with little hand painted flowers and vines. Asha and Glenda were seated in overstuffed chairs in the corner, each sipping tea out of dainty teacups. A wrought iron round table sat in the direct center of the room and it was loaded with food.

I salivated as the smells hit me. Two days was a long time to go without food and I was definitely ready to eat.

"We weren't sure what you would fancy, so we had Bev over at Buoy 6 whip up a little of everything for you. Ronnie sent over mimosas and told me to tell you she is at your disposal as you get settled in."

I nodded and moved around the table to survey the options. Enormous fresh baked muffins, a dish full of fluffy eggs, a plate of crispy bacon, hash browns, pancakes, heck —there was even a fruit sculpture. I wanted it all and had a brief crisis over where to start.

In the end, my hunger won out and I just piled some of

everything on the plate. Asha motioned for me to join them in their nook and produced a bright yellow tea cup out of thin air.

"Earl Grey?" she asked, "Or are you more of a coffee person?"

Tears actually pricked my eyes as I stared at her. "Earl Grey, please," I breathed, sitting down hard and jamming a piece of muffin into my mouth.

"Ohmygod," I mumbled around the bread, "Thif if so good."

Glenda peered at me from over her teacup and smiled. "Bev outdid herself this morning. She loves to bake. Misty Cove considered it a lucky day indeed, the day she settled here. Best kitchen witch on the West Coast and here she is in Misty Cove making muffins!"

I couldn't speak. I was too busy having a spiritual moment with baked goods. I managed a nod, and both Asha and Glenda smirked at me.

Swallowing hard, I looked at them sheepishly.

"Can we just forget the men and maybe the three of us form a matesbond? We can ask Bev to join us. Can we be the baked goods pod?" I asked, hopefully.

Asha burst out laughing. Her slight frame almost disappeared into the chair as she convulsed. Glenda looked at me with amusement and sipped her tea, shaking her head.

"You're a beautiful woman and I love Bev's muffins more than the average person but, alas, I fear my mates and child would have something to say about my abandoning them for a new ladylove." Asha finally wheezed.

"And I don't think you should give up on those boys yet, dear. I can't speak for the Leprechaun, although he looks vaguely familiar, but the other two are wonderful men and I think they may surprise you. But, if you want to be part of our sewing circle, you're more than welcome." Glenda added with a twinkle in her eye.

"I don't think I know how to sew," I answered glumly.

"Oh, that's alright, dear. It's not that kind of circle. Ronnie calls it Stitch & Bitch and very little sewing gets done. She started it after she'd been here for a while to 'escape the dicks' in her household. A few of the other women in town who are in pod and pack relationships joined in. It's a great opportunity to meet people here in town and we banned the men."

"Uh, girls night? I am so in. I don't even know if I have girlfriends back in Las Vegas. It's a little weird, right? That I might have a whole other life somewhere and I just... don't know. Belfast says he knows, but I can't remember a goddamn thing."

Asha and Glenda both set down their tea and patted my knees gently.

"I have some tonics I want to try, to see if we can get a cause for the brain fog," Asha mused. "I suspect it has something to do with the crystal you carried that suppressed your shifter side. Depending on how long you carried that, your koala could have been so worn down and diminished that she was fighting for survival. The shift and the car accident could have put her in fight-or-flight mode and she's preventing being muted again until she's strong enough to survive."

I ate some of my bacon and tried to work through that in my head. It was so strange to imagine my koala nature. I had no recollection of ever being a koala, and I did not know how to even get in touch with that side of myself.

"Did the crystal hurt her?" I asked, dreading the answer. I may not know my koala very well, but I wasn't a monster who wanted to have her hurting.

Glenda looked sad.

"Your koala is part of you, she depends on you for survival. Your shifter heritage is the reason you're healing so fast. Magic can shut her out, but it was never meant to work like that. Shutting her out with the crystal would have been highly stressful for her and you. It's like, severing your heart from your soul. You can't exist without each other, although you can try for a while."

I felt like shit. Somewhere out there, I or someone else had given me a crystal that had caused my koala immense pain.

The idea made me feel sick inside and my stomach clenched. I set down my half-empty plate, I couldn't eat when I felt like this.

What kind of person was I in real life? Someone who would willingly hurt one side of myself?

A clatter at the front door made me jump, and my plate dumped onto the tiles with a sharp clatter.

Glenda waved me off when I knelt to clean up the shattered plate and Asha waved her hand and muttered an incantation that caused the whole mess to fly through the air and land neatly in the trash can.

"Whoa. That's seriously impressive," I stared wide-eyed at her.

She smiled and sipped more tea. "You know, you probably could do that, too. You have magic. I can tell. It's not weak either."

I bit my lip and tried to concentrate. Just like it felt impossible to feel my koala, I couldn't manage to feel my magic. It was like the brain fog had spread to all my limbs.

A deep booming voice from the foyer carried into the sunroom, and I recognized Frank's voice. A small bloom of something exciting started in my core and I rose to greet him.

He ducked under the doorway and looked so wholly

out of place in the delicate, feminine room that I almost laughed. Holding an honest-to-god cowboy hat in one hand and a giant bouquet of flowers in the other, he looked supremely uncomfortable.

"These are for you," he thrust the flowers into my hands as soon as he saw me.

I staggered under the weight of the arrangement and inhaled the sweet fragrance.

"Um, thank you!" I managed, moving the enormous arrangement to the side table and standing awkwardly in front of him with my hands in my pockets.

"I'm just.. I think I left a crystal charging overnight. Must check that." Asha hurried out of the room with something that looked suspiciously like a smirk on her face, leaving Frank and me to stare at each other.

"Do you want any breakfast? Perhaps some tea?" I finally offered, gesturing towards the remains of our breakfast buffet.

Frank nodded, saying nothing, and stalked towards the table and grabbed a plate. I watched, open-mouthed, as he built a small mountain of food, piling huge scoops of everything into one colossal serving.

Damn. Bears eat a lot. Should I ask him if he's hibernating? Is that rude?

His hands were almost as wide as the breakfast plate, and I shivered again from awareness. *What is it about those hands? Is it because they are just so big? You know what they say about gigantic hands... God, I wonder... I wonder what they would feel like wrapped around my...*

"Little Bit, what are you thinking about?" Frank interrupted my inner reverie with a pained look on his face. He was standing stock still and his breathing was labored. His eyes were wild with just a tint of the bear-yellow I saw previously. *Whoa. That's hot.*

79

My face flushed red, and I mumbled something under my breath before turning to find my tea cup.

I sensed him as he moved behind me and I almost forgot to breathe when he gently touched my shoulder and turned me to face him.

"Um, tea?" I chirped brightly.

Frank said nothing. He just stared into my eyes, the intensity rolling off him and pooling in my core.

I probably should have been scared. A giant stranger had cornered me and was staring me down, but I wasn't remotely afraid. Nope. Fucked up brain or not, I felt... *Excited. Really excited.*

This felt oddly... right.

"You're so damn beautiful it hurts," Frank finally whispered, his voice low and husky. His words filled my heart and I bit my bottom lip and looked up at him through my lashes.

Frank was intense. Frank was a stranger. Frank saved my sorry ass on the side of the road. And, for reasons I didn't fully understand, I really, really wanted Frank to be... mine. I could almost imagine a tie between us, an invisible link to each other.

Was this the Matestone magic? Ronnie had assured me it was always my choice and the Matestone just kind of took away the awkwardness to show you the chemistry.

Well, check the chemistry box for Frank. Check it hard... and often.

I swallowed hard and took a small step towards him. I wasn't even sure why, I just wanted to touch him. I *needed* to touch him.

Slowly, he reached down to caress my face with his calloused hand and I leaned into it, rubbing my cheek into his touch like a cat. His thumb traced the outline of my lips with such exquisite softness that I feared I might melt.

Yep. Chemistry.

Closing the distance between us, I took the last step into his embrace, shyly wrapped my arms around his waist, and hugged him, laying my head on his chest and sighing in contentment. He froze for a brief second before his thick arms wrapped around me, locking me into his embrace.

I could hear his heart pounding and his masculine pine scent flooded my nose, threatening to overwhelm whatever shred of self-control I had left.

The feel of him. His scent, the way he held me so tightly and so carefully... it was doing things to me.

I leaned into him and pulled him tighter to me, burying my face in his shirt.

He ran his hands up my sides, resting his palm on the back of my head and caressing my hair gently. Each touch felt like a brand on my skin, claiming me and drawing me in closer. My back arched in response to his touch and I swayed slightly on my feet. A little moan escaped me when he gripped the back of my neck.

His chest rumbled, and he dropped his hands, cupping my ass and hoisting me up. I screeched in surprise, but instinctually wrapped my legs around his waist and looped my arms around his neck.

He carried me across the room until we were at the only wall without a window or bookcase. Pressed up against the wall with his impressive hardness rubbing against my aching core, I gave in.

"Frank," I breathed, flexing my thighs so I could rub against him even more. I wanted to purr like a cat, I was so turned on.

"You are incredible," He whispered, cupping the side of my face with a frantic look on his face before he captured my lips in a blistering kiss that set my soul on fire.

I let myself fall into him and lost myself in the magic

of his kisses. When his teeth scraped my neck, I moaned and nibbled on his shoulder, making him growl in approval. When he slid his hand up my shirt to cup my breast, teasing my nipple until I cried out, I trailed my hands down his side to cup his ass, pulling him harder against me.

At first, I didn't notice the telltale signs. The goosebumps and the prickling feeling under my skin. By the time I did, it was too late.

When he bit my lower lip and unbuttoned my shorts, I stiffened, arching against him and flailing my arms.

"No, no no no," I cried out, tears springing from my eyes.

Frank froze, carefully easing me down the wall to stand before him and stepping back with his hands up and clearly off me.

The pain rocketed through my body and I convulsed in a heap on the floor, my bones shortening and the tips of my fingers fusing into the claws. When the white-hot pain seared into my skull, I let myself scream.

Glenda and Asha came running into the room, ready to defend me. Frank looked horrified, standing helplessly to the side, his face still flushed from our intense makeout.

Then, as suddenly as it started, the pain was over.

I lay on the floor panting, a thin layer of grey fur covering my arms and little fuzzy koala ears sticking out from my purple hair.

"I think I was just cockblocked by my fucking koala," I whispered, curling up on the floor in a ball. "Frank, I'm so sorry. I'm... a freak."

I burst into tears and hid my face behind my arms, curling even tighter into a ball.

I felt Frank move to stand next to me, and the thud as

he slid down the wall to sit down. Gently, he stroked my hair.

"Never a freak, beautiful. Your animal has just been through a lot. That's all. We pushed her too far today and she lost control. It happens. We'll figure this out together. I promise."

Glenda and Asha murmured over my head somewhere and I felt something cool lay across the back of my neck.

"Kalena?" Asha called out gently, "We need to get you back to bed. It's going to take a few hours to get the tonic ready to help you shift back if you can't do it on your own."

"I've got her." Frank's voice rumbled.

"Little Bit, may I carry you to your room?" he asked sweetly, his stubble caressing the top of my ear.

"Sure" I whispered faintly.

We didn't speak as he scooped me up and carefully carried me to my room. Gently depositing me on top of the bed, he spread a lap blanket over me and kissed my forehead.

"We're going to find answers for you, sweetheart. I promise."

Asha and Glenda ushered him out, closing the door behind them, leaving me alone in the room. Alone and fuzzy.

With tears in my eyes, I pulled at the fur growing in my arm, howling in pain when I managed to pluck a few hairs back.

"You're a bitch," I whispered furiously to my koala. "No wonder I kept you locked up."

A dull pain radiated out of my chest and I doubled over, gasping as it intensified and my vision tunneled.

The Matestone coin glowed a deep purple on my

bedside table and I gasped again in pain. My back felt like it was breaking.

What was wrong with me?

"Help?" I whispered faintly before my eyes rolled back in my head and toes fused into claws.

The last thing I heard was Glenda yelling for Asha before I fell back into the blackness.

Chapter Nine
Belfast

Kalena was here. I had found her. She had the *Anam Cara*. It was safe. By all counts, I should be celebrating. The mission was a success.

In one night, I had saved my own ass and found the one person on this plane of existence that I really, truly cared about.

So why wasn't I more excited?

Because she's your mate, dumbass. And turning her in as the thief of the Anam Cara is not exactly a courting gift, it's a death sentence.

I kicked a rock on the sidewalk in frustration and watched it bounce across the road and land next to the neatly landscaped building with a sign over the entrance that read *Misty Cove City Hall*.

Misty Cove was a fascinating little sliver of the world. An entire town filled with supernatural residents. I'd heard that these little enclaves existed in the human plane, but I had never come across one as big and as well-run as Misty Cove. Usually the enclaves were nothing more than a poorly run commune with a couple of packs that were trying to scrape an existence out of the dirt.

But this was a proper town. It had government services,

charming little businesses, and… a bar somewhere that was run by the only other Matestone Guardian the world had seen in centuries.

A pale woman walking along under a black, ruffled umbrella gave me an appreciative look on the street, her eyes lingering on my pecs. I flexed for her out of habit and her eyes turned red and her fangs popped out. *Oh. Succubus. Lovely. Perhaps I should magick up some actual clothing for town…*

"Hello, stranger," her voice was soft like velvet and I could feel the power behind it. Custom required supes to withhold their powers when greeting another supe and for once, I was thankful for tradition and ritual. This succubus was clearly powerful, maybe even a coven leader.

"Hello!" I greeted her cheerily, letting my power rise to the surface and watching passively as she felt it and nodded her head in acquiescence.

"You're new here," she pointed out, twirling her umbrella over her shoulder and sidling up close to me. "You may call me Venice."

"Ah yes. My mate and I are visiting," I replied lightly, emphasizing the word mate with as much energy as I could. She raised an eyebrow when I failed to give her my name and smiled at me with blindingly white teeth and pointed fangs. "Excellent. I look forward to meeting them. We love visitors here in Misty Cove."

"Maybe another time. I was actually hoping to find a place called Buoy 6? Could you point me in the right direction?" I stepped slightly away from her and remained on guard. There was something about her that made me uneasy. Succubi and Incubi were not uncommon in this realm. Gods knew there were more than a few that worked at Lucky Charmz. But I got the feeling that this one didn't hear the word no very often.

She pointed me down the road and left me to my own

devices. I walked as quickly as I could, but as I did, my skin crawled with unease.

That one was trouble.

When I finally found the bar, it was packed with people. Cars and motorcycles lined the parking lot and the street in front. There was even a horse tied up to the railing of the verandah. Boisterous groups sat out on the patio, overlooking the ocean while servers hurried back and forth carrying heavy trays of beer.

Apparently Buoy 6 was the place to be in Misty Cove.

I was attracting a fair amount of attention in my Club outfit. With a wave of my hand, I magicked myself into a dark pair of jeans and a tight white t-shirt with some jaunty aviator sunglasses. As long as no one looked too closely at my glittery skin, I would blend right in.

I took a deep breath and walked in, determined to seek answers about this Matestone business from the only person I knew who could provide them.

Inside, people were packed into booths and tables, and the volume was impossibly loud. Off to the side was a small hole in the floor with a ramp and a railing built around it. A selection of robes hung off one hook next to the ramp. I watched incredulously as a harbor seal flopped up onto the floor and shifted effortlessly back to human form. She wrapped herself up in a robe and went off to join her friends. The only evidence that she had just come from the literal ocean was the small trail of wet footprints and the fact that she was sitting in a bar in a bathrobe.

Supernatural culture was typically very nudity friendly, but the way Misty Cove accommodated ocean shifters was something I hadn't seen before. It was seamless and welcoming, and it made me even more thankful that places like this existed for them.

I guessed it took a Matestone Guardian mated to a pod

of sea lions for that kind of architecture to become important.

"Can I help you, hun? Table for one?" A perky server interrupted my staring, and I shook my head. Her name tag read "No" and it made me do a double-take.

"Uh, I'm not eating. I am here to see someone named Ronnie about a thing called a Matestone?"

Conversation around me stopped, and gradually, everyone in the dining area turned to stare at me. *Well, so much for staying out of the spotlight.*

"Uh, Ronnie?" the server yelled, not taking her eyes off my face.

The woman in question extracted herself from an embrace with one of her mates and came over to where I was trying to melt into the floor. The server whispered in her ear and the woman's eyebrows arched impressively.

"You've got a helluva way of making an entrance," she remarked, looking me up and down. "Let's get you in the back before we have a riot."

"Earl," she yelled over her shoulder, "send Chuck over to the house and tell him we'll meet him there."

The largest man in the group waved his hand in acknowledgement and stalked out the door to head towards the pier. I stopped walking and stared at her.

"Yo, Sparkles, I wasn't kidding about the riot. You waltzed your fine ass in here and said the word Matestone. It's kind of like Jumanji… that word has power. Unless you want to put your little friend on the menu for every Tomcat, Dickhead, and Furry out here to try for her until your bonds have been solidified, you'll listen to what I have to say. We're headed to my place. It's safer to talk there."

I grinned at her sass and followed her out the door. We weaved in and around patrons, Ronnie occasionally stopping to greet a few people and answer questions. Glenda had told me that she had only been in town for a year. It was very clear that she had spent that year becoming quite the local fixture.

Once we were free from the patio seating area, Ronnie beckoned me to follow her and we headed towards a gated yard full of motorcycles. A youngish looking man with an eyepatch and a leather vest was leaning against the gate.

"Howdy, ma'am," he saluted Ronnie and moved to swing the gate open for her. When I stepped forward to follow, he put his hand out.

Ronnie rolled her eyes and grabbed my arm and pulled me through. She threw a wink to the guard, "This one's with me, Pax. Earl will fill you in."

"Uh, what is this place? Are you a local business owner, restaurateur and... mob wife?" I asked, looking around at the casual but alert stance of all the men in the yard.

They were at ease, but their eyes were glued to me and I knew if I so much as looked at Ronnie wrong, I was going to have a bigass problem.

"Mob wife? Psh. No. More like Old Lady to a motor-cycle gang. If that motorcycle gang was totally into coaching softball, helping me run a restaurant, and providing town security."

I nodded in appreciation, eying the flagpole in the middle of the yard and wondering exactly what this gang of motorcycle-loving sea creature shifters would do to me if I took that pole for a spin. *Probably kill you, dude. Just keep your clothes on for a hot minute.*

Dancing had been my escape. Ironically, flying kept me grounded emotionally. The strain on my muscles as I pushed myself to do more daring acrobatics, to stretch my limits and the roar of approval from the crowd, night after night. It was the closest thing I had to emotional support and here, in the middle of an emotional maelstrom that had no hope of ending anytime soon, I missed it.

"Come on in and have a beer. Chuck is on his way. At least one of my pod is home, yell and you might find the rest of them!" Ronnie yelled over her shoulder and gestured towards an open kitchen area.

I was just cracking open a beer when Chuck walked through the door and gave me a head nod in greeting.

"Ronnie said you were in here." He stated, digging in the fridge and pulling out a plate of cheese and cold cuts.

"Here I am." I took another sip of the beer and stared at the butcher block counter.

Could this be any more awkward?

Chuck didn't answer me for a long moment, he just kept building his sandwich like he had all the time in the world. Which he did.

"I have questions," I blurted out, earning myself a raised eyebrow from Chuck as he nodded and licked the mustard off his finger.

Three burly men came pushing into the kitchen, loudly arguing about a starfish and Chuck and I froze. They greeted Chuck with gusto, punching his arm and giving him shit. But when they turned to me, the jovial attitudes were gone. Instead, three steely eyed sea lion shifters stared me down, and I actually felt a brief twinge of fear.

"I hear you almost caused a riot down at Buoy 6," the middle one said. A patch on his vest read *Trevor*, and I gulped.

"Nah, he's fine, guys. He knew Kalena before she came here. I think he's just worried about her." Chuck jumped in, motioning for me to grab my beer and follow him out onto the deck.

Gratefully, I nodded to the rest of Ronnie's harem and moved towards the door.

"Hey Leprechaun," one of them called. I turned back to face them.

"We take our protection detail seriously. Ronnie is a Matestone Guardian and it sounds like your friend, Kalena is too. You *will* respect her and you *will* take good care of her or we will be forced to kick your shiny, golden ass back to whatever pot of gold you crawled out of."

They all marched out of the kitchen before I could respond, and I laughed shortly. I was 546 years old, and I just got threatened by sea lions who probably weren't even 50. Technically; I had access to more power than they could ever dream of having but I vowed long ago not to tap into my family heritage unless it was to save my life or that of my loved ones. Besides, their sentiment made me weirdly happy.

They didn't even know Kalena like I did, and they were willing to protect her. She was an intensely private person, but over the years, I had learned that she had had a shitty upbringing with parents who refused to accept her as a shift-witch. She could use as many people in her corner as she could get.

"Don't let them bother you. They really aren't that bad, they just get a little tetchy with newcomers." Chuck leaned against the railing and stared out at the ocean.

"Eh, it's understandable. I was a dumbass and my words could have made a sticky situation for their mate. I get it."

Chuck nodded, finishing his sandwich before turning to look at me. The sun was setting and the golden light played across his pale hair. He and Kalena would look striking together.

"You're staring, dude," Chuck raised his eyebrow at me and I forced a chuckle.

"I never get used to being called dude. It's such an

endearing term of address. I was only thinking that you and Kalena would look good together, that's all."

To my surprise, Chuck flushed bright crimson red and took a huge swig of his beer before violently choking and spilling the bottle all over the deck.

"Whoa!" I stepped back and reached for a beach towel to throw at him.

"Sorry, I just. I don't know how to talk about Kalena with you. Or them. Or anyone," he started, looking intensely embarrassed.

"I mean, you just met her a couple days ago. That's fair. She's still working on getting her memories back and dealing with her fuzzy side. But, maybe tomorrow I could ask her if I could help fill in some gaps for you and Frank? Give you some tips on what she likes or dislikes?" I brushed his hand with my arm and sent him a small dose of my calming energy.

Leprechauns got the weirdest gifts in Faery. We got shiny objects, rainbows, hoarding, and the ability to minorly influence human emotions. *And the Anam Cara. Can't forget that.*

Chuck studied me for a minute, looking me up and down as if he were assessing my worthiness. He sighed heavily. "Maybe you should offer that to her, too, just in case her memories don't come back."

The idea of Kalena being stuck in this strange world of amnesia was sobering, and I turned to watch the waves off the deck. She was my best friend. *I will help you remember, a stor, I promise. Even if I have to remind you of our stories every day.*

"Look, man. I don't know a lot about the Matestone. I didn't grow up with my pod, so the lore wasn't passed down to me as a child like it is in some families. I just know what we've learned as a Club with Ronnie here. Fate chooses Guardians and they have to be protected, cherished, and treasured. The Guardians choose their mates. I know, without a shadow of a doubt, that Kalena is my mate. I would choose her right now if I could. But it doesn't work that way. She has to choose me, too and I just... I don't know that she will. There are a lot better looking guys out there for her. I mean, look at you." Chuck continued, clearly oblivious to my change in mood.

I fought the urge to hug the younger man who was so clearly hurting.

"Well, doesn't the Matestone thing mean multiple mates? Why are you counting yourself out? You defended her and let yourself get punched in the face. While Frank and I were measuring dicks, you were looking out for *her*. Do you know how much gestures like that mean to her? She's had to scrape by on her own for years. She's not used to people looking out for her. I think you're ok."

Chuck stared out over the water pensively and processed the words I had said.

"Do you want to get out of here?" He asked suddenly. "Like, hit up a bar outside of town, get kind of plastered, and just... try to make sense of this? I mean, if she chooses us, we're gonna be brothers for life, man."

A sense of unease and hope warred within me. True Mates were rare among the Fae and even rarer among the Leprechaun Clans. My people usually arranged a marriage for political gain and paid others to have our children. Nothing that would distract us from building our wealth and hoarding gold was permitted. A love match? A match endorsed by Fate herself?

Virtually unheard of.

I had been drawn to Kalena for a long time. Her energy called to me, and I had dreamed of her; longed for her.

The fact that something like a Matestone could give me

what I never allowed myself to dream of... I scarcely dared hope it was true.

"Yeah," I turned to Chuck, "Getting plastered sounds perfect right about now. And dancing. Let's go dance."

Chuck laughed a little and drained his bottle of beer and pitched it perfectly into the recycling bin in the corner of the deck.

"Let's go, brother." He clapped my shoulder and went inside, returning with a jacket and hat.

"Are we taking your ride or mine?" he asked cheerfully.

I grinned at him. I so rarely got to show off my unique portal skills, and I had a feeling Chuck would get a kick out of it.

"Ever traveled by rainbow?" I asked, carefully drawing the runes with a pencil on the porch.

Chuck looked slightly terrified. "Uh, nope. Haven't done that. Is that... safe?"

I laughed and opened the portal, calling my rainbow light to me and relishing the feeling of my powers stretching within my soul.

"Perfectly. Do you trust me?" I offered my hand, and he hesitated for a second before stepping into my portal.

"Where are we headed, *Mo dheartháir*?"

"The Hydra! Just outside of town?"

Together we vanished, riding the rainbow light across the bay, and landing gently on top of a knoll next to an old lighthouse.

Chuck staggered as he stepped out of the portal and leaned against a tree for support.

"That was wild." He looked pale and slightly sick.

I just grinned. The beat of the music at the bar down below was thumping in my veins and the urge to dance was almost overpowering.

I looked down at the clothes I was wearing critically. They wouldn't do for the kind of movement I wanted.

With a grin, I waved my hand and changed into skin tight leather pants and a bright green t-shirt.

Chuck stared, eyes wide. "Whoa, that's a helluva party trick," he joked, heading down towards the party.

I ran to catch up and threw an arm over his shoulders.

"You've no idea the kind of party tricks I am capable of," I teased, "I'm a *Leprechaun, Mo dhearthāir*. It's what we do!"

Together we descended down the hill and joined the throng of people dancing the night away.

I almost cried when I saw the giant silver pole set up on stage. My blood buzzed in my veins in excitement.

"Wanna learn to dance?" I asked Chuck, pointing towards the pole on the stage.

He turned bright red and shook his head no, and I just laughed. The night was young. The drinks were flowing. Yeah. Misty Cove was fast growing on me.

Chapter Ten
Frank

S he was naked on the bed, propped up on her elbows, watching
me. Her hair, still damp from her shower, hung loose around her
shoulders, the curls springing every which way. A picture of perfect
purple chaos standing out against her pale skin. She looked so beautiful there, surrounded by pillows of every shape and size. Smiling at
me, she beckoned me to come closer while she patted the soft throw
pillow next to her and ran her hand through her hair, shaking it out.

My bear growled in approval. Our mate was finally home in our
den. It was the moment we never allowed ourselves to dream of, and
yet here she was. A soft den for our perfect, beautiful mate.

"Frank," she called out, spreading her legs and arching her back,
enticing me to come to her.

Raw, wild need flowed through me, begging me to claim her. But
I needed it to be perfect, so I stayed just out of reach, prowling around
the bed so that I could check every detail of my den.

She watched me hungrily, her grin playful and inviting. My heart
slammed into my chest each time I looked at her and my cock
throbbed.

Meeting my eyes with a knowing grin, she leaned back and ran
her fingertips down her body, caressing the skin I longed to touch.

My self-control was slipping and my bear demanded we seal our bond. *Nevertheless, I held back. She was the sunshine in my life, the one who had brought joy and laughter back to me when I never thought it would return.*

What did I bring to her? A den? Years worth of baggage?

My heart beat faster, and I looked away from her. Could I make her happy? Could I be what she needed?

A soft hand touched my shoulder, and I whirled around. My mate, my beautiful mate, was kneeling in front of me, concern etched across her perfect face.

"Frank, you're overthinking this," she said softly, framing my face with her tiny, delicate hands. I let my forehead fall forward to rest against hers. She looped her arms around my neck and held me, our hearts beating in sync for that perfect moment.

I wanted to be everything for her. Her protector. Her partner. Her lover. Her mate. But I couldn't trust myself not to lose control. My need for her made me almost brutal with desire. My hands shook from the effort not to touch her.

She deserved better. A lover who was gentle, not one who was half-mad with desire.

My bear wasn't soft and cuddly. He was savage with lust.

"I trust you," she whispered in my ear, her hot breath tickling my ear, "and I want you, Frank. I want you so much I ache." She reached down and grabbed one of my hands and dragged it down her body, stopping just inches from the apex of her thighs.

"Feel how badly I want you, Frank. How badly I want you to claim me." She whispered as she dragged my fingers over her slit, using my fingers to pleasure herself.

My breath was ragged, and my control was perilously close to breaking. With each stroke and satisfied sigh, she broke away a little more of the armor that I had put up.

"Frank," she pleaded, leaning back and pulling me with her.

I knew I should walk away. I should never have let it get this far. But I let her drag me down and then her lips found mine and the last piece of armor cracked in two.

I pulled away from her, growling as I pushed her back further into the den. With a roar, I ripped my clothing off my body. She watched me with lust in her eyes, not fear. As I stepped out of my jeans and threw them in the corner of the room, her chest heaved and she bit her bottom lip, squirming in anticipation.

"No more games, Frank." she whispered breathlessly, "I want to be yours."

I pounced on her, pinning her to the bed with her hands above her head. The bed creaked, trembling underneath us. Her curves molded to fit my body, and she met my hungry gaze, writhing underneath me and threatening to undo me even more.

Pinning her wrists with one hand, I reached down, finding her soaking slit once again. Without warning, I slid two fingers into her, stroking her hard and deep.

She arched into me, crying out as she crushed her lips to mine. The touch of her mouth was greedy and possessive and I reveled in it, but my bear demanded I take back control. Nudging her knees further apart with my thigh, I let my weight pin her down deeper into the soft mattress.

"Stay just like this," I ordered, releasing her hands to trail my hands down her luscious curves, stopping to nibble on her rosy nipples before peppering her body with kisses, tasting every inch of her.

When I lowered my head to the juncture between her thighs, she gasped and thrashed against me. I scraped my teeth against her soft skin, making her squirm and wiggle in my grip. When my tongue teased her, working her folds and swirling around her sensitive nub, she arched into me, her hand coming down to grip my hair and hold my head in place.

"Do not stop, Frank. Don't you dare stop," she whispered, her body taut with need and anticipation.

My tongue worked her while I slipped one finger into her, and then two, stroking her faster and faster until her whole body tensed and clenched around me. She let out a low moan and convulsive waves wracked her body. I wrenched my mouth away from her and pumped my fingers, keeping the rhythm while I popped up to my knees. Quickly withdrawing my hand, I plunged my aching cock into her until I was fully sheathed.

I leaned forward, balancing on my elbows. Brushing the hair out of her face, I looked down at her and pressed a searing kiss to her lips.

This was my mate.

My love.

The one Fate chose for me.

"I claim you, Kalena," I whispered, positioning my teeth over the soft part of her shoulder.

"All that I have is yours. All that I am is yours. All that I—"

RING.

RING.

RIIIING.

I sat straight up and looked around, my heart racing and my body drenched in sweat. My phone was ringing. Disoriented, I looked around and let out a heavy sigh.

I was at home. Alone. My cock was throbbing and hard as steel while my goddamn phone rang endlessly.

With a growl, I swiped the small device off the table.

"This better be a life or death emergency, emphasis on the death." I snarled into the phone, gripping my cock with one hand and stroking firmly.

The other line was silent for a long moment, and I felt my rage building. If I was interrupted out of dream-claiming my mate because of a prank call, someone might actually die.

"Frank?" A small voice finally spoke, and all the blood drained from my face.

"Kalena?" *Shit. Shit. Double-fucking-hell.*

"Yeah, it's me. Um. I just. Can you come over?" She asked.

I swallowed a groan and willed myself to get back under control.

"Of course, Little Bit. I'll be over in a few minutes."

"Thanks. I'll, um, unlock the door." She hung up, and I sat back and looked down at my twitching cock.

"You're gonna make this easy and come quickly, right?" I asked my member, glaring down at it while I stroked myself. "We've gotta go see our girl and we can't exactly go armed like this!"

I tried to go back to my dream, imagining my mate beneath me while I drove into her, sheathing myself in her warmth and wetness while I sank my teeth into her neck. Claiming her.

A few strokes later, my dick was spent and my heart was racing.

My bear had already claimed her. I was claiming her in my dreams. The kind of need I had for her was almost as strong as my need to breathe, to eat, to hunt. It was intrinsic to who I was. And that scared the motherfucking shit out of me.

With a sigh, I cleaned up and picked up my keys and jacket. My mate needed me.

THE CLINIC WAS dark when I arrived, and I parked my truck on the side street and walked up to the front door. Sure enough, Kalena had left it open for me. I made a mental note to have a talk with her about safety tomorrow.

Misty Cove was a safe place, but with an unclaimed Matestone in play, all bets were off. I remembered the hubbub that happened when the local wolf pack tried to kidnap Ronnie. I doubted my bear could be as forgiving as the sea lions had been if that were to happen to Kalena.

I crept through the dark clinic and stopped in front of

the guest bedroom. The light peeked out through the door and my pulse started racing again. I knocked gently.

"Kalena? It's Frank," I called quietly.

"Come in," she answered. Steeling myself with admonitions of self-control, I pushed the door open.

A wave of pheromones and arousal hit me like a ton of bricks and made me take a step back. *Stay cool. Stay in control.*

Kalena was sitting up in bed. She wore a thin tank top and her hair piled on top of her head. Her face was flushed, and she blushed even further when she saw me.

"Are you ok?" I asked, standing just out of reach of her with my hands firmly in my pockets.

"Um, yes and… also no," she offered meekly. She patted the edge of the bed and scooted over to make room for me to sit down. "If you mean, am I fuzzy? No. Asha fixed that for me. If you mean, am I ok emotionally with this whole Matestone-Fated thing? Also, no. I'm kind of freaking out. But, I got a few of my memories back. Just a few. I know a little more about who I am."

I clenched my teeth and willed my dick to cooperate and not fuck this up for us, or worse, make it excruciatingly weird. The fact that my mate was confiding in me meant she trusted me. I would rather die than give her a reason to question that trust.

"Oh yeah? What did you learn?" I asked, seated gingerly on the bed and actively avoided looking at the swell of her breasts underneath that very thin tank top. *Fate is testing me. Be cool.*

Kalena looked uncomfortable and picked at a loose thread on the bedspread. "So, I'm half witch. My parents are actually leaders in their coven, but we… don't talk. They're the ones who kept me from my shifter side. They were ashamed. I remember that clearly."

My bear rose within me and snarled, angry on her behalf that a part of her was rejected by her very parents.

"I am so sorry, love. No wonder you don't know how to control your shift. No one ever trained you. Do you... want to talk about it?"

She hesitated for a moment and then shrugged.

"From what I can piece together, my initial childhood was quite privileged. But my entire identity was shattered the night I found out I was part shifter. It was dinnertime. I honestly don't think they would have ever told me, except I partially shifted and freaked out. Then... everything just blew up and they came clean."

My heart broke for her, and I draped my arm around her shoulders.

"I remember they told me so calmly. Like it wasn't a grenade they were casually dropping into my life. Between soup and the entree, I had partially shifted into an animal, learned that I was the product of a fling, and was told I would likely be a low-magic witch. I was also warned to never, *ever* tell anyone about what I could do. They didn't ask me if I had questions or give me any other information. They just... told me. Then rang the bell for dessert."

I hugged her closer to me, my bear wanting desperately to protect her and take all the pain she had ever suffered away.

"It probably would have been fine except..." Her voice caught and she turned toward me. "I got outed. A classmate told the council. It was a big thing. Witch bloodlines and all that. A huge scandal for my parents. Long story short... I left home when I was fifteen and they didn't look for me or try to bring me back."

A frown marred that perfect face and I ached for her.

"That's not all, though. One of my family powers is uh, rather unusual." She blushed a beautiful pink, and I cracked a smile. She was so damn cute when she was blushing.

"What kind of unusual power?" I prodded, curiosity eating at me.

She met my gaze and then dropped her eyes to my lap. "Dreamwalking, Frank. Our family power is dreamwalking."

I got a head rush.

The smell of her arousal that permeated the room? The way I dreamed of her? What we shared?

"What are you saying, sweetheart?" My voice was so low it sounded like a growl.

"I'm saying, you called out for me in your dream, *Frank*. And I followed it and... I broke the rules."

My entire body tensed up. *Broke the rule? What the fuck does that mean?*

"I, uh, got *involved* in your dream. I broke the rules and kind of... joined in."

I stopped breathing for a second while I tried to process that. I had been woken up from the most intensely sexual dream of my life by my mate who was not only the star of said dream; she was also the voyeur. *That... That may have been the hottest moment of my life.*

"I didn't ask you and that's just a huge violation of your privacy and I'm sorry," she said contritely, looking down at her hands.

My brain stuttered as she apologized. "No, there's nothing to apologize for. Did you want to join in? Did you... like what happened in my dream?" I asked, holding my breath and clenching the bedspread in my fists. *Moon Goddess, hear my prayer.*

"Are you asking me if I liked the dream dick you gave me?" Kalena asked, her eyes sparkling with amusement.

I exhaled and met her gaze. "Yeah, I guess I am."

She giggled again before scooting over on the bed so she could touch me. "Frank," she began, framing my face with her tiny hands and giving me a sense of deja vu. "That was one of the sexiest moments of my entire life. I've never had dream sex before and you were magnificent."

My cock rose to half mast at her words and my bear felt like strutting, but I forced myself to sit still on the bed.

"What do you think would have happened this afternoon if I hadn't, you know, koala'd out? Why do you think that keeps happening?" She asked wistfully.

I inhaled sharply and looked at her.

"I don't know what happened with your koala this afternoon, babe. Maybe she just needs a little more time to heal. But I know I want to spend a lifetime proving to you just how much I want you and need you. I shouldn't say this but, after what we shared in our little dreamwalk, I think I can." I took her hand and brought it to my lips.

"I know you're my mate. My bear knows it, too. I don't deserve this kind of happiness. One day you'll know why, but... I'm a selfish sonofabitch and I can't leave you. Not until you decide."

"Stay with me, Frank?" she asked, scooting over and pulling aside the covers. "Just to sleep. I don't want to be alone."

I slipped off my shoes, stripped down to my boxers, and slid under the covers. She turned on her side and backed up so her back was flush against my chest and her ass was nestled right over my crotch.

I draped my arm over her and held her close, listening as her breathing evened out and soft snores left her nose.

Lying here wide awake with my sleeping mate pressed up against me and a raging hard-on that I had no ability to take care of was just about as close to perfect as I ever thought I would have.

"Good night, my love. My mate." I whispered in her hair, pressing a kiss to her ear.

Easing my phone out, I shot off a text to Chuck and Belfast and gave them an update. *We're a pod already. This is our future.*

Belfast texted me back a picture of him and Chuck swinging around a pole in a crowded bar, and my bear growled in warning. Those two dipshits were at *The Hydra*? They looked drunk off their asses. *Unacceptable.*

Kalena stirred next to me as I typed out a furious reply for the two to get back here. Glenda and Asha had moved Kalena to the larger guest room at the clinic, complete with a small sitting area and an ensuite bathroom. There was enough room for all of us.

I carefully propped myself up against the headboard of the four-poster bed and settled in to watch over my mate while I waited for the rest of her pod.

Chapter Eleven
Kalena

I t was hot. Like inferno-hard-to-breathe hot. I cracked my eyes open and struggled to take a deep breath. A hairy arm was draped over my chest, pinning me securely to the side of a very large, hard, naked chest.

"Ok," I squirmed, trying to get comfortable, but froze when my ass rubbed up against something else very large and hard. *Oh my. Good morning, indeed.* I wiggled my ass again, just to be sure. *Yes, this IS a good morning.*

Giving up on securing my freedom, I focused on the lump on my couch. It was electric green with bright red hair. "Belfast?" I croaked, squinting.

It was definitely Belfast. He was asleep, his head leaning back over the edge of the loveseat and Chuck was fast asleep curled up on the other side, his legs across Belfast's lap. It was, quite possibly, the cutest thing I had ever seen.

I would have been quite content to watch them sleep except I was burning up and moving Frank was like moving a boulder.

"Frank," I hissed, squirming again, causing him to grip me tighter and pull me into his chest.

"Ugh. Men."

My bladder made it very clear that I could ignore those needs at my peril, so I tried again to ease myself out from under Frank's bulk. Frustrated, I pushed at his arm but he just groaned and snuggled in tighter.

"Freaking velcro teddy bear!" I grumbled, my ass brushing up against his morning wood again and awakening yet another set of specific needs.

An evil idea came to mind, and I carefully scooted closer to Frank and wiggled my ass against him. He moaned, and I grinned. *Game on, teddy bear!*

Slowly, deliberately, I slipped my sleep shorts down off my legs and kicked them off at the foot of the bed. With only a thin piece of lace between us, I ground my ass against Frank's bulge and rocked my hips against his.

The moment his breathing changed, I grinned. *Good morning, sunshine!*

He shifted next to me and his arm drifted south, finally unpinning me and letting me take a deep breath. I inhaled gratefully and wiggled my butt again for good measure. *Positive behavior rewards!*

His fingers danced across my thigh, caressing my soft skin as he pressed a sleepy kiss against the back of my neck, sucking on my pulse point.

I moaned. The second it escaped, I clapped a hand over my mouth in horror.

Belfast stirred but didn't sit up. Chuck was still snoring. *That was close!*

I tried to wiggle away from Frank and creep out to the bathroom, but his teasing fingers locked me in place the moment I tried to escape his clutches.

"Just where do you think you're going, temptress?" he growled in my ear, nibbling on my shoulder and making my entire body shudder.

"Bathroom," I hissed back, swatting at his wandering hands playfully.

He reluctantly let me up, leaning over to press a sloppy kiss to my lips.

"Good morning, beautiful."

A silly smile spread across my face and I leaned over and kissed him on the nose.

"Good morning, yourself!"

I eased out from under the covers and padded carefully past Belfast and Chuck to the en suite bathroom.

After freshening up and brushing my teeth, I carefully slipped out and tiptoed back towards the bed where Frank was laying, looking at his phone.

A hand snaked out and grabbed me around my waist, pulling me into the couch heap.

"Ahhh!" I shrieked as I fell onto Belfast's lap.

Frank looked up and smiled at me before pointing his phone at us and taking a picture.

"Do I get a good morning kiss too, *a stór?*" He asked cheekily. I giggled and turned to straddle him. Chuck had woken up with my screech and pulled his feet back and was watching us with bleary-eyed interest.

With all three of them watching me, I suddenly felt emboldened and excited. The three of them were supposed to be my fated mates, and they were 100% into sharing. Why shouldn't I take that lifestyle out for a spin and see if it worked for me? *It's only responsible to try before you buy. Everyone knows this.*

Sinking down onto Belfast's leather covered lap, I rocked against his bulge and bit my lip as the friction increased. Leather and lace sliding against each other was a delicious combination. His eyes flashed a brilliant green and his hand anchored my hip onto him, pushing me down to grind harder.

I gripped his arm for balance, rolling my eyes when the gold glitter dust came off and covered my hand.

"Does your dick sparkle too?" I asked suddenly.

Chuck burst out laughing, and Belfast sputtered.

"I mean, does it glitter? Like your arms and the rest of you?" I just had to know.

Belfast surged up and pressed a blistering kiss to my lips, his tongue diving in to tangle with mine, tasting and demanding I forget anything other than the way he felt under me. Then, just as suddenly, he pulled away and lifted me off his lap. Gently, he put me down on Chuck's lap and stepped away.

"I will have you know, my dick is impressive enough without needing extra sparkle!" he boasted, magicking away his clothing to reveal a very impressive, very erect cock.

I licked my lips, locking that image away in my memory before nodding my head at Belfast and turning back to the matter at hand.

Chuck.

My sweetest protector.

The one who had my back 100% of the time. I didn't even know what Chuck *was*. I think he was a shifter, but it didn't matter. He was mine, too.

"Good morning, Chuck," I whispered, wrapping myself around him. Frank made me feel like nothing could ever get to me. Like he would stand between me and hell itself and I would always be safe. Belfast made me feel desired and wild. The way he looked at me made me feel like the sexiest person to walk this cursed planet. But Chuck? Chuck made me feel cherished. He made me feel like someone who deserved to be treasured.

In less than a week, these three had wormed their way into my life and I couldn't imagine living without them.

"Kiss me, Chuck?" I whispered as I ran my fingers across his shoulders.

His beautiful baby blue eyes sparkled as he brought my face down to his and pressed a warm kiss to my lips. His lips were petal soft, tasting and teasing me, brushing against mine before dipping lower to tease me with a few soft kisses on my neck.

Each time I tried to deepen the kiss, he pulled back, smirking at me and reestablishing control.

Chuck's gentle touches and maddeningly soft caresses built a fire in me that threatened to explode into an inferno. I lost myself in his touch and the exquisite game he played, building me up slowly and then drawing out the pleasure until I was almost panting and ready to beg him.

"Chuck," I moaned, quivering under his latest touch.

"What is it you want, sweetheart?" he asked, sucking lightly on my earlobe and making my entire body shake.

"Do you want me? Do you want Belfast? Do you want Frank? Do you want all of us?" He peppered kisses down the edge of my jaw and I rocked against his erection eagerly.

"Yes," I moaned. "Yes, I want all of you. Together. Separate. I just want all of you. Preferably now."

Chuck looked over my shoulder and then over at the bed, clearly having some sort of non-verbal guy conversation.

I took advantage of his distraction and rubbed myself further against his bulge, seeking the release I so desperately needed, but fearing that it would, once again, be ruined by the unplanned emergence of my koala.

"On the bed, sweets. We want to worship you properly. All of us, together. So you know what that's like." Before he could finish his sentence, I had my mouth pressed to his in a searing kiss. My arms locked around his neck and I devoured him with a hunger that surprised me.

He met me with unbridled passion, gripping me hard against him, his tongue dancing with mine. When he finally pulled away, we both had glassy eyes and swollen lips.

Two more sets of hands reached for me, helping me off Chuck's lap and leading me to the bed. I quivered in excitement and almost fell flat on my face, but they caught me, keeping me safe.

One after the other, they took turns kissing me while the others played with my hair or stroked my body, caressing me with hands and lips until I felt like I was floating on some sort of cloud.

"Gods, this is the life," I gasped as Belfast dove between my legs and ripped the lacy thong underwear off with his teeth before devouring me, his tongue driving me absolutely bonkers.

"This could be our life, if we are a pod," Chuck offered in between sucking on my nipples and leaving little love bites on my chest and neck.

"Mmm. What a life it would be, too." I murmured dreamily, tilting my head back so Frank could kiss me.

Belfast rubbed my clit with his fingertip while he worked me with his tongue and I could barely breathe from the heady mixture of pleasure, anticipation and fear of my koala.

My orgasm built slowly, the pleasure shooting through me with each touch from each of my sort-of-mates. I teetered on the brink, hovering over the edge until Belfast curled his fingers, rubbing against my G-spot and forcing me to cum.

The rough motion sent me over the edge and my toes

actually curled as I came. Three waves of pleasure crashed over me before I felt the first tingle.

"Oh no, oh no. It's happening again," I gasped, "Let go of me, all of you!"

Six hands left my body, and I immediately felt their loss. Every nerve-ending in my body quivered, this time from pain. Tears streamed down my face as I convulsed and shifted, my body, once again, stopping mid-shift and forcing me to remain in the in-between stage of human and animal.

"Goddess, help me," I cried out, anguish tinting my plea.

"I've got Asha and Glenda and one of the senior coven leaders on the way. His name is Timoteo and between all of us, we're gonna fix it, sweetheart, I promise you." Chuck leaned over me and kissed me on my mostly human forehead. As if he had summoned her by word alone, Asha appeared in the doorway. Her bright pink hair was sticking up every which way and her clothing was mismatched.

As she fed me the foul-tasting tonic that would force me to shift back, she watched me with a look of deep concern on her face. Glenda and Timoteo waited, holding crystals up with alternating frequencies and whispering incantations.

I chugged it and waited.... And waited..... And waited... A few hairs disappeared on my arm and my clawed extremities slowly shifted back, but the ears on my head and the fur on the rest of me lingered. One thing was for certain: my koala wasn't going away without a fight.

I glanced around the room, and Asha and Glenda were looking worried, as were Belfast and Chuck. It made me uneasy.

Frank quickly threw some clothes on and kissed me,

hollering something about needing to see someone about a solution as he thundered out the door with a slam.

"Ok, guys. What aren't you telling me? I demanded once I could catch my breath again.

Asha pursed her lips and shook her head, and Glenda patted my arm.

"I honestly am not sure. I need to do some more research. I haven't seen a case like this before—I'll keep you posted!" Asha muttered, examining the notes on her clipboard as she swept from the room.

Belfast and Chuck exchanged a look and then climbed into the bed with me.

With one on each side, sandwiching me between them, I felt my heart rate finally start to calm.

"We're not going anywhere, sweetheart." Chuck whispered as he pressed a kiss to my cheek.

"*A stór*, you are everything to me. To us." Belfast vowed, bringing my hand up to his lips for a sweet kiss.

I let them comfort me, settling into their warm embrace and snuggling closer. As they held me, my mind raced.

Memories, disjointed and incomplete, flashed through my brain, along with the fear that if they—these beautiful men of mine—knew who I was, they would run for the hills and never look back.

How could Fate choose someone like me? An Academy dropout and magical misfit who couldn't even control a basic shift.

Chapter Twelve
Chuck

Our poor mate was suffering, and I was powerless to help. I couldn't imagine what it would be like to be so disconnected from my dolphin that I couldn't shift all the way. To feel trapped between two worlds. The pain that Kalena experienced while shifting was excruciating to watch.

Frank's connections were extremely deep, and I hoped he had run off to someone who could help us. It was strange that Kalena's inability to control her shift seemed to be tied to her strong body feelings like arousal. I had never seen something like that.

We were all concerned.

In all my years living in Misty Cove, I had never seen Asha and Glenda look this worried about someone. It made my chest hurt. No shifter could exist without a harmonious relationship with their animal based on love, care, and mutual respect. It was physically impossible.

Yet, each time Kalena partially shifted, a portion of her memories came back. It was the strangest thing. But each partial shift was also taking longer and longer to undo, almost as if the koala inside her was learning how to adapt.

It wouldn't surprise me. Koalas are very resourceful when they need to be.

Kalena was tucked under Belfast's arm, and he was stroking her hair. Her breathing was even, and I motioned to him I was going to get up. He nodded, pulling Kalena tighter to him and draping his leg over her body.

We would keep her safe or die trying. Matesbond or not, the three of us had been brought together by Fate to protect this woman. I was certain of that.

I stepped out into the hall and Glenda met me with a cup of coffee and a fresh chocolate chip cookie.

"How are you holding up, dear?" she asked, patting my shoulder comfortingly.

"The same as the rest of us, I think. Confused? Worried?" I munched on the cookie and looked out the window at the Main Street shops.

The streets were busy today; so many people going about their daily business as normal. Glenda made the best chocolate chip cookies in the Pacific Northwest. They were slightly crunchy on the outside, chewy on the inside and charmed by Asha so they never got chocolate stains on you or your clothing. *And they say witches can't solve world problems!*

"We're moving her to the apartment over the apothecary this afternoon. She is healed and we need the bed. " Glenda sipped her tea.

"No! She's not well! And the Matestone? She won't be safe!"

Horrible scenarios ran through my head of Kalena getting kidnapped by rogue shifters or dying in the apartment as a half-shifted koala.

"She's a grown woman, Chuck. I expect she's kept herself alive all on her own without you for some time. If the apothecary apartment doesn't work, there are others available."

There were apartments available all over Misty Cove. One perk of having a powerful, very active coven in town was that housing was never an issue. As long as there was a tree willing to act as an anchor, the Oak Tree Coven had figured out how to create sustainable and movable mass housing using a combination of pre-fab homes and treehouses.

I paced the room, my mind working through all the different scenarios.

"She's staying with me." I snapped.

It was the perfect solution.

"I have room for all of us in my bungalow. That way, she could be protected, monitored, and she would have her own space if she wants it. I'm right on the beach, the waves might soothe her."

Glenda gave me an indulgent smile and handed me another cookie.

"Very well. If she agrees, I will plan for her things to be moved over to your bungalow this afternoon."

I smiled tightly and handed her my coffee cup. If my mate was moving in today, there was work to be done.

MY BODY practically buzzed with nervous energy. I never truly thought I would get the privilege of moving a mate and a pod of my own into my house, and now that it was happening, I surveyed my domain with a critical eye.

My mate was moving into my home. Today.

Holy shit. This is actually happening.

I never stopped moving. I straightened pillows, tossed clutter into unused closets, and swept endless piles of sand out of the entryway. If my MC Club guys saw me, I'm sure they would give me shit about nesting. And they would be right. I *was* nesting.

It was silly and vain, but I wanted Kalena to fall in love with my home as well as me. I couldn't give her riches like Belfast or paramilitary-style protection like Frank, but I could give her a home to lounge in and make her own.

If she wanted it.

If she *chose* us.

The airy, four-bedroom bungalow had been my passion project every weekend for the last five years. I had a permanent room at the Sea Lion MC Clubhouse, but every weekend after my shifts were done and my duties complete, I would come over here and lose myself in the building project. There was always something that needed adjusting, tweaking, or changing to make it perfect.

Floor to ceiling windows in the living room had an unrestricted view of the ocean and each of the bedrooms had been expanded so they could all accommodate a king-sized bed and a walk-in closet. The deck was wide and expansive, big enough for a small party to gather on without being disturbed... or for a small pod to lay out under the stars together.

A little tingle of awareness and desire spread through me, and I gulped. *A Pod.*

Kalena. Frank. Belfast. And... *me.*

Belfast had promised to watch over our mate while she napped and then bring her over to the house after lunch, and now she was due to arrive at any minute. I looked at the clock and quickened my pace. A car door slammed outside, and I ran a hand through my hair.

She was here.

I ran out to greet her and pulled her into a tight hug.

Kalena's gasp of surprise when she entered my home was everything I could have possibly wanted. She gushed over the minor details and hugged her arms to her body in childlike delight.

"I can't believe you actually live here!" she exclaimed. She stood at the edge of the living room and gazed out at the deep blue sea.

"Oh my gosh, is that a whale out there? Chuck, come tell me!" she pointed excitedly at the window and the distant spouts of water showing a whale pod.

I grimaced in disgust.

"Yeah, probably. We've had a lot of whales come through lately, they're migrating. Don't worry. They won't be out there long." I looked out at the expanse of water and felt resentment that the whales had dared to interfere in *my* paradise.

"This is for you," I held out my hand and she took the small dolphin keychain and key from me with a smile.

"Are there dolphins here?" She asked, running her finger over the smooth texture of the plastic toy.

I puffed up a little and squared my shoulders.

"There are a few around. The only Guiana Dolphin on the West Coast lives here, too!" I winked at her.

She pursed her lips and turned to look back over at the bay.

"I always wanted to see dolphins in the wild." she whispered longingly.

It took every ounce of self-control I possessed not to shift immediately and flop myself down the beach so she could get her wish. Pride filled me at her obvious enjoyment of dolphins.

"Is there a special time of day to go out and see them?" she asked, still staring at the wide expanse of the Pacific Ocean in the distance.

"Oh, I think you can see the dolphins whenever you

want," I laughed, "I could even arrange for you to swim with one."

"Shut up, really?" I had her full attention now. "I could seriously swim with dolphins here? There's a marine park? Where is it?"

A look of horror crossed my face.

"Marine park? What, like an aquarium?" I asked, scandalized, "That's barbaric! We would never do that here."

She flushed red and mumbled something about it being a joke. It was on the tip of my tongue to tell her I was offering to let her swim with *me* because *I was a dolphin*. But Belfast caught my eye and waved me off, his eyes sparkling in mirth. I frowned at him and then shrugged my shoulders.

"Let me show you to your room so you can get settled," I led her from the room and towards the bedroom suites.

She ran ahead, squealing in delight over each thing, and I watched her fondly.

"Dude, time that right. You're a fucking *dolphin*. Show that off. Take her out to the pier at sunset or something and get her hyped up to swim with the dolphins and then swan dive that shit into the ocean and let her freak out all over you. Trust me. She's going to be so into that." Belfast clapped my shoulder and then turned off to one of the guest rooms.

"Nice place, by the way. This one ok for me?" he asked, his hand hovering over the handle. I nodded and he disappeared into the room without another word.

Smiling to myself, I followed the sounds of Kalena's squeals while she explored the room that I had set up just for her.

Yep. Having a mate in the house was the best.

.⁺·ᴜ⁺·

WHEN BOTH KALENA and Belfast disappeared into their respective rooms, Belfast to change and Kalena to "shower in that rainforest shower until I turn into a prune or a fish," I was at a loss of what to do with myself.

My guests had arrived, been properly greeted and were, presumably, quite content with their accommodations. My dolphin was restless, and I looked longingly at the ocean outside my window. I hadn't shifted in several days and I was craving the salty spray of the ocean and the taste of fresh-caught fish.

It would be beyond rude to leave my houseguests while I ran away to play in the sea. "We have to stay here, for our mate," I whispered to myself, trying to talk some sense into my dolphin.

My dolphin was torn. The desire to be close to our mate warred with our instinctual need to be in the water.

Glancing back at the empty hallway, I pulled my shirt off over my head and walked down the steps toward my pool.

It wasn't the ocean, but it would do the job.

The cool water felt amazing on my skin and I dived deep, shifting underwater and racing from one end of the pool to the other. When I built this place, I made sure it was twice as deep and twice as long as a regulation pool. With water filtered directly from the sea, it was as close as I could get to the ocean on days when I couldn't make it down the beach.

My dolphin leapt out of the water and chirped, diving back down and racing around in excitement. Before I could fully stretch out my flippers, something soft and fuzzy hit my head and I dove deep, aiming for the furthest reaches of the pool.

Shifting back while underwater, I surfaced carefully and looked around for the intruder who had so rudely interrupted my swim. *That asshole is about to get a lot more than they bargained for, too.*

Belfast sat perched on the edge of the pool holding a foam football with a shit-eating grin on his face. From this angle, he looked bare-ass naked. Which, to be fair, so was I.

I sighed and brushed my hand over my face in irritation.

"Kalena's taking a nap," he offered, pitching the other football deep into the pool.

"Ok," I gritted out, trying to remain calm. My dolphin was pissed at the interruption and the water called to me.

Belfast dropped into the water and swam easily over to where I was.

"So. Whatcha planning for her?" He asked, floating lazily on his back next to me. I was relieved to see he was wearing a swimsuit, even if it was a barely there speedo.

I didn't know what to say. I hadn't planned any further than getting her moved in, which was now completed.

Belfast read the distress on my face and placed a reassuring hand on my shoulder.

"BBQ, man. We'll set up the grill and we can all sit out on your party porch. I know what she likes."

I nodded. BBQ would be good. I could get some fresh fish, I had beer. It would be fine. Having Belfast here to give a frame of reference to Kalena's life before Misty Cove was really helpful.

"You can go back to swimming," Belfast offered, kicking against the side of the wall and floating away from me. "I just wanted to see what we were doing. I didn't mean to intrude."

"No, wait. Maybe you could tell me a bit about what she likes?" I hoisted myself up out of the water and sat on the edge of the pool. "Or maybe you could tell me how you first got her to notice you?"

Belfast looked thoughtful.

"I danced at the club she worked at. Night after night, I'd swing my body around the pole and dance for these screaming humans. Brides, mostly. She kind of tried to blend into the background, but I always saw her. She was kind and beautiful and sassy as all hell. She hated the spotlight, but I would see her swaying to the music, night after night, and I always wondered what would happen if she would let herself be free." Belfast splashed around the pool a little more, drifting back towards me.

"She was my friend, Chuck. She still is. Always will be. I've... done things in my past. Even got myself banished from home. My sister phones me from time to time, but I can't go home. Maybe that's why we bonded at first. Kalena was banished, too."

I sucked in a breath and leaned forward to listen. Kalena's memories were coming back faster, thank the Moon Goddess, but her history was still a giant question mark.

"Her parents threw her out when people outside the family discovered she was part koala. She's been on her own for years. When I met her at Lucky Charmz, she was like a breath of fresh air. She never judged me for my past. She just accepted me."

Belfast looked up at me with unshed tears in his eyes.

"I've been alone for 150 years, Chuck. Banished from my home and ostracized by my kind. The only one that even talks to me is my sister, and that's only once in a blue moon. Before I met Kalena, the only solace I got was when I was dancing. Now, Matestone or not, I don't think I could stop loving her if I tried. My kind, we don't do fated mates per se, not like shifters, but we have the legend of the True

Mate. Kalena is mine. I know it. I just wish I was a better person for her sake."

Belfast's naked honesty surprised me, but the vulnerability he felt, the way he didn't think he was good enough of her—it was relatable.

"If you love to dance so much, why don't you dance for her tonight? At our BBQ?" I asked him, diving into the water with ease.

Belfast grinned, "Aye, I'll dance for her tonight. I'd dance for her every night. But what if you joined me? She'll be out for another hour or two. What if I taught you how to dance for her? We could double up."

As he winked, a strange sort of excitement shot through me and I nodded.

Belfast waved his hand, and a small pile of clothing appeared on the pool deck.

"Go get dry and dressed then. Lessons start in five."

I climbed out of the pool and picked up the tiny pair of shorts and the glitter body spray with trepidation.

What did I get myself into?

Chapter Thirteen
Frank

The pier was crowded and my bear resented each time I was forced to dodge a family with a stroller or a pack of feral children running around. *Our mate is in trouble! Nothing else matters. Run these people over. Force them to move!*

But I couldn't. Misty Cove was my home, and these people were my neighbors. My friends. My community. They couldn't possibly know the fear in my heart, each time I thought of my mate and the suffering she continued to endure. How could they? Between Ronnie and her mates and Asha and Glenda's discretion, we had kept Kalena mostly a secret. To the best of our knowledge, no one even knew another Matestone was active in their midst. These were just families and fellow Misty Cove supes enjoying the late afternoon sun in our idyllic beach hamlet.

My height put me at a head taller than 90% of the crowd and I could spy the familiar faded yellow and blue building immediately when it came into view at the very end of the public boardwalk. Hope bloomed in my chest and I hurried towards it. With any luck, it would house the answers we so desperately sought.

There was something wrong with Kalena. I knew it. My pod-brothers knew it. Other than the glittery one, we were all shifters. We knew intimately the animal bond and the compulsion to shift, to work in tandem with both our natures.

Kalena's animal was not well. Or perhaps she was divorced from it entirely.

The idea of being divorced from my bear caused a jolt of pain in my heart that almost dropped me to my knees in the middle of the crowd.

It wasn't right.

Even with only one shifter parent, Kalena still had her animal and clearly the ability to shift, even if she didn't communicate with her koala-side regularly. To be repeatedly stuck in a painful partial shift wasn't normal nor healthy.

Asha's working theory was that Kalena had been subjected to some sort of spell that lived in the magically charged crystal we found in her bag. This spell would have had to be extremely powerful to suppress half her nature for years.

Spells like that were usually only ever used with Council approval and only when the shifter hybrid in question was at risk of extreme harm. To use it for years to suppress a healthy shifter was a gross misuse of power.

Glenda was sure the absence of the crystal and the partial-shifts that occurred when Kalena was feeling powerful emotions indicated her koala was getting stronger. But I wasn't ready to take any chances. Not with her. In one week, she had gone from a stranger to my entire world.

One week ago, I was just Frank. I drove a truck, delivered supplies to other supernatural communities, and kept to myself. It wasn't a terrible life. It had worked for me for a long time.

But it was a lonely life. My bear whined in my chest.

Now, I was on the cusp of everything I never let myself dream of. A mate. A pod of my own. A *family chosen by Fate.* My priorities had shifted dramatically over the past week.

What if she doesn't choose you? Look at her. She's in the prime of her life. Why would she choose a washed-up has-been like you? The snide little voice in the back of my mind tortured me and my bear growled, scaring a small family next to me.

The Matestone rules were clear. No matter how I felt. How much I knew in my heart that Kalena was my mate. She had to willingly accept the matesbond.

I tried to tell myself that it had only been a week and Kalena had experienced a significant amount of trauma.

It wasn't like she had accepted matesbonds from any of the other men in the pod. Glenda and Asha said it looked like we had some time before the Matestone forced the choice.

But… there was no guarantee. It was early. She could choose an entirely different pod once we got her koala sorted out, and it would be 100% her right to do so. Decisions like that were final.

Please, Moon Goddess, let her choose me. Let me claim her as my mate.

But even with the possibility of a heartbreak that might destroy me, my resolve was firm. Kalena was the center of my existence, as was the possibility of our family.

There was nothing I wouldn't do to protect my family.

I jogged the rest of the way down the pier and wrenched the dirty glass door open.

Misty Cove Marina & Charters.

It wasn't much to look at, much like your typical coastal property. The paint was peeling from too many storm seasons spent being salt-blasted by the waves and spray. Inside, the lighting was dark and the pervasive smell of fish still permeated the air.

I scanned the crowded room for the one person who could give me answers: Moray.

It was hard to see with the dim lighting and the floor-to-ceiling displays full of brochures advertising coastal tours and trips. The hammock in the back corner was empty and panic seeped into me. *What if he wasn't here?*

"Moray! You around?" I called out desperately, checking behind the desk and warily eyeballing the semi-hidden trapdoor down to the water that was installed when Moray first took possession of this property about twenty-five years ago. There was no answer, and I tapped my foot on the worn wooden floor.

Moray was one of Misty Cove's more... *unique* characters. Everyone knew of him, but few people claimed to actually know him and for good reason. For a person whose job relied on interacting with other people, he genuinely preferred to be alone most of the time. If he didn't *feel like* talking to you, he wouldn't. Then there was the matter of the sheer amount of power that just roiled off him like a cloud. Most people kept a respectful distance.

I still vividly remembered the day he arrived in town twenty-five years ago. Just walked out of the surf one day, plunked down a literal bag of gold, bought Old Man Henry's bait shop, and settled in.

I was still a teenager and mostly preoccupied with raising hell. The mystery of the wild scion of the sea who had moved in on the pier was too enticing to pass up. My buddies and I plotted and planned a spy mission to find out more about our strange neighbor. For two weeks that summer, we built out plans and speculated what we might find.

By that time, the rumors had already taken hold. Some people in town thought Moray was an heir to lost Atalantean royalty, others were convinced he was a demigod or spawn of Poseidon. A few speculated he was a criminal or pirate or hiding out from the Oceanic Council.

Being the arrogant asshole of a cub that I was, I'd volunteered to be the one to break into the building that fateful night and get our first look inside. The night we chose was stormy—a late summer squall had blown in and the wind and rain beat down on us. The entire town was content to hunker down and wait it out. It was perfect.

I made it to the pier that night and took up my observation post. Everything looked abandoned and empty. When I made my move, I thought I was hot as shit. I rolled up to the window full of the arrogance of youth. Shifting my hand, I clawed at the window on the door and broke it open. The thunder and lightning hid the noise of the glass breaking and emboldened me further.

By the time I had unlocked the door and crept inside, I felt like I was on the top of the world.

The interior of the building back then didn't look much different than it did today. I ruffled through the paperwork scattered on the desk and snatched a few of the brochures I found to take back to my buddies as proof of my reconnaissance.

Maybe Moray would have let me get away with it if I hadn't taken it one step further.

I found a permanent marker lying on the desk and scrawled "Sea Freak" over the top of the desk. To this day, I still don't know what possessed me to do that. Vandalism was never my style. But that night... That night, I wanted to show this newcomer that Misty Cove was *my town*.

I never saw the shadow move.

One minute I was standing in the doorway, the next minute I dangled from the trapdoor- the angry chasm of the stormy ocean and rocks and pilings below waiting for me.

"Hello, bear. You aren't in the right place, are you?" A soft voice sounded in my ear. Moray didn't have to raise his voice to scare the piss out of someone. The soft, almost gentle question made all the hair on my body stand up and I struggled to free myself, reaching desperately for my bear.

But Moray's magic was powerful, and it easily over-powered me. I couldn't see what held me suspended over the water, but I was scared shitless. Moray let me struggle, holding me in place until I was drenched and shivering uncontrollably.

I had never known fear like that before. When he forced me to remain unshifted, my bear actually hid and left me. It didn't take long for me to honestly believe I was going to die.

I begged for his forgiveness. I pleaded with him to let me go for hours while the storm raged around us. But he never answered me. Eventually, I stopped trying. Resigned to my fate.

It was only the next morning, as the sun was rising, that Moray finally pulled me back up.

"You will stay for tea," he ordered quietly when I collapsed in a heap on his floor. I was too terrified to do anything else, so I agreed and sat in the furthest corner of his shop and shook from cold and fear.

Moray handed me a delicate gold-rimmed teacup that said "White Star Line, HMS Titanic" on it and my hands shook when I took it.

The tea warmed me instantly.

"Where I come from, an invasion and desecration of

territory is punishable by death." He sipped his own tea and stared at me pensively.

"Why didn't you kill me last night?" I asked after a long moment.

"Because I am tired of killing."

We sat in silence that morning, sipping tea as if we were old friends until he finally stood and held his hand out for my teacup.

"I will accept your help in cleaning up this mess you've made as well as additional labor to repair my building as restitution for your incursion. You will ensure that there are no repeat occurrences, my young bear friend. I cannot promise such restraint next time."

I worked for Moray that entire summer.

In his own terrifying way, he'd made me who I was today. As time passed, we formed a sort of friendship. He never spoke about the incident again, nor did he speak of his past. When he opened the Charter business, I helped him navigate the town council process and smoothed over his lack of social graces. When I was spiraling out of control following the freak accident that had taken my sister's life, he was the one who got through to me and sent me to serve in the Army.

Together, we had forged an unlikely alliance. The headstrong young bear and the ancient powerful creature. I had my suspicions about what he really was, but I would sooner die than bring it up with him.

Today, I needed him more than I ever had before.

"Moray, please! I need your help. I found my mate and…. she needs you. I need you!" I called out, sinking into the metal chair next to the door and resting my head in my hands.

The *squeal* of the trap door hinges got me to lift my head.

Dark blue eyes the color of the deepest ocean blinked at me from the dark, and I smiled in relief. At least he was willing to hear me out.

"Young Frank. I daresay you do not require my assistance in claiming said mate, do you?" Moray asked as he hoisted himself up through the trapdoor and stepped out of the shadows and into the light.

Shifters age slower than average, but every time I saw Moray I was struck by how frozen in time he appeared. He reminded me of a sea-based vampire. Tall, pale, secretive, and strong. He moved with the grace of water and his voice wound its way into your psyche like a siren's song.

"She's a shifter who can't shift. Or, rather, she can, but it doesn't work. She has no connection to her animal at all. Half the time, she says she can't even feel it unless she's about to partially shift. And her partial shifts? They're brutal and painful for her, like the animal is fighting for survival instead of working with her human side. I don't know what to do." All my worries, my uncertainties, the questions I had—I let it all out.

Moray nodded sagely and moved to sit in the large hammock he kept in the shop's corner and dried his pale blonde hair with a towel.

"Was there magic involved? A spell of some sort?"

I shrugged. "There was a crystal that repressed the shifter side that was found in her belongings, but other than that, we aren't sure. She was in an accident and her memories are still a bit scrambled."

"Perhaps time will be the greatest of healers for your fair mate, my friend. I do not know what I could do. I am not a healer," Moray said gently.

Time.

Desolation ripped through me. I couldn't go back empty-handed only to tell Kalena that this was it. I couldn't tell her that there was nothing I could do. Patience didn't seem like something she would be good with. It definitely wasn't something I was good with. And this was no way for any shifter to live. I couldn't stand the thought that she was destined for a lifetime of excruciatingly painful partial shifts. Moray wasn't a healer, but he wasn't powerless.

I took a deep breath and put all my cards on the table.

"You have more power in your pinky than this entire town combined, Moray. We both know it. I'm begging you. *Please*. There has to be something you can do. Even if it's just information. Anything."

Moray looked thoughtful, and then he picked up his phone and punched in a series of numbers that seemed far longer than the average telephone number.

He smiled as the line clicked.

"Bill, a friend of mine requires your help rather urgently. Yes, a portal would be fine." He spoke quickly and then ended the call, hung up the phone to look at me again.

"A friend of mine might be better suited to assisting you. He will be in shortly."

Before Moray had even gotten all the words out, a portal opened in the center of the room. It glowed with black fire and I leapt out of the way just in time.

A man dressed in a long, purple, paisley-printed silk robe and holding a small container of popcorn, stepped out. It took me a second to realize that horns protruded from his forehead. They were tipped in gold and a sudden shock of recognition jolted through me.

Bill was Bilexphiles? The notoriously fickle ancient forest demon? What the -

"What's crack-a-lackin, my friendly neighborhood

Kraken?" Bilexphiles joked as he tossed a piece of popcorn in the air and caught it in his mouth.

I stared at Bill before glancing at Moray, who grimaced and nodded, corroborating the casual claim.

Kraken?

Wait.

THE mythological Kraken with a capital K?

Holy.

Shit.

I cleared my throat and caught the attention of the two most powerful beings in our entire community.

"It's my mate, sirs. She needs help..." I began.

Chapter Fourteen
Kalena

There were few things more satisfying than a nap. I couldn't remember if I'd always loved naps or if this was a recent phenomenon, but naps are fucking awesome. Especially naps that left you feeling refreshed and in possession of some more memories.

Glenda made the observation that it was probably because koalas sleep 18-22 hours a day in the wild, and now that I was getting up close and personal with my koala side, I would probably be exhausted all the time.

She wasn't wrong.

Goddess bless Google search for the helpful info.

The house was quiet and the late afternoon sun warmed my skin as I stretched languorously on the bed and then pushed myself to my feet. Life at Lucky Charmz Club played in my head like a movie. I remembered Belfast, his dancing antics, and the way his skin gleamed when the light hit it just right. *Belfast was fucking delicious.*

I pulled a light sundress out of the backpack Asha had given me and changed into it quickly. Once I'd swiped some mascara on my eyelashes and pulled a brush through my hair, I decided I felt more sort-of-human again and padded off to find my boys.

Once I concentrated on visualizing the threads that were embedded in my heart, connecting me to each of them, it wasn't hard to find them. The individual threads glowed on their own and had a distinct vibration. The thread that led to Frank was a brilliant navy blue, strong like the man himself. His wasn't glowing as brightly so I guessed he wasn't nearby. Belfast's was a blinding golden color. It radiated warmth and playfulness.

I tugged it a little and was rewarded with a small jolt directly in my nether bits. *That's a fun game. I'll have to remember that for later.* Chuck's connection was a sea-foam green color. Steady and soothing. He radiated happiness and something else. I couldn't put my finger on it.

The closer I got to the deck, the clearer I could hear the steady pulse of club music bumping in the background. It was familiar, and that was comforting.

That has to be Belfast.

I bounced along with the beat and sashayed out to the kitchen. Something smelled delicious, and I was definitely ready to eat.

But the kitchen was suspiciously empty, so I meandered out towards the deck and the source of the music.

Skidding to a stop in front of the floor to ceiling windows, I watched as Belfast rubbed some sort of sparkly oil on Chuck's chest while they both laughed.

The sun was making Belfast practically glow golden, but this time Chuck was gleaming, too. They both were shirtless and wearing impossibly tiny green booty shorts, like the kind Belfast wore to the Club to dance.

Belfast threw his head back and gyrated his hips in time with the music and then stopped, gesturing at Chuck who hesitated before attempting the same motion.

The two of them thrust and gyrated with the beat, gleaming in the sun like two hedonistic sun gods. Belfast leaned back against the deck railing and pointed towards the chair. He was explaining something with lots of hand movements and I watched in rapt attention as Chuck nodded seriously and then sat in the chair with his legs set a shoulder's width apart.

The music changed to Pony, and I had to stifle a giggle, ducking down behind the counter so they wouldn't see me. This was better than HBO, and Pony was one of Belfast's *jams* at the Club.

Peeking up over the counter, I watched Belfast move behind Chuck. He flung his arms up and rotated his hips, bringing his palms down to slap his own ass. Strutting forward, he circled the chair to face Chuck and leaned forward and caressed his cheek before dropping into a squat and then stepping forward, straddling him while gyrating his hips again.

I couldn't take my eyes off them. I'd seen Belfast dance hundreds of times before, but this was the first time I'd ever seen him work his magic on another guy. It was surprising, but also… incredibly sexy. Halfway through the song, he pulled Chuck close, and they swapped places.

Chuck stumbled through the first beat but he caught it, dropping and locking like a pro before returning to straddle Belfast and awkwardly hump his leg. It was surreal. And also quite possibly the sexiest thing I had ever seen. A naughty fantasy popped into my brain that involved the both of them, a chair, a bottle of tequila and me. *Is that the way pods work? Do the guys get involved, too… with each other? Do we do group things with everyone getting in on the action? That's kind of awesome. I have so many questions.*

Where Belfast exuded an over-the-top, overtly sensual persona all the time, Chuck was naturally more reserved.

Seeing him like this, raw and passionate as he committed to this… chair dance, or whatever the hell it was… it was mesmerizing. The music ended, and I felt torn between announcing my presence and waiting to see what other shenanigans they might get up to.

Chuck offered Belfast his hand and pulled him up out of the chair and into a casual embrace. They thumped each other on the backs in that quintessentially bro-like way before dancing over to the BBQ and cracking open beers.

It all seemed so… wholesome. If two of your mates stripping down and practicing sexy dance moves on each other while grilling on the deck could be wholesome.

Belfast said something to Chuck and gestured towards the house and turned to come in. I panicked, opening cupboards as if the only logical option was to hide. In a cupboard.

The sliding door opened and Belfast walked towards the fridge, whistling along with the music. I crouched down out of sight and painstakingly crab-walked my way backwards towards the hallway.

My concentration was so focused on avoiding Belfast and the unavoidable conversation of my spying that I failed to hear the slider open again. I bumped directly into Chuck and fell over in a heap.

Blinking, I looked up from the floor and was temporarily blinded by the sheer quantity of glitter-covered muscles that were leaning over me. It was like a fantasy dream-sequence I never wanted to wake up from.

"Kalena? Sweetheart, what are you doing on the floor?" Chuck asked, offering me his hand.

I bit my lip and mumbled something nonsensical under my breath, accepting his help to stand up with the absolute minimum level of grace.

This was humiliating.

"What was that, *a stór*? Are you ok?" Belfast asked, studying my flaming face with amusement.

I stood awkwardly between them and felt myself over-heating. Each time I looked at them, my mouth got a little drier and I felt like I was sweating.

"Ok, fine! I saw you, ok? I saw you and I couldn't stop watching and then you came in and I hid because I didn't want to catch me spying and for the love of the Moon Goddess Herself can I get a bottle of water?" My words rushed out in a jumble, I stared straight at the floor in front of me. *I am the world's most awkward person. Was I always this way or is this something new from the shifting and lost memories?*

Both of them were silent for a moment. One blissful moment of silence.

Then the laughter.

Chuck was actually crying. Belfast was howling, glitter falling off him in little puffs each time he slapped his thigh, which was A LOT.

I stood there between them and watched as they completely melted down into hysterics.

"Kalena, *baby*, you're our mate. Or, well, we'd like you to be. You can always come see us. It's not spying. If that were you out there dancing, you'd bet your fine ass I'd watch, too." Belfast finally managed, wiping tears from his face in amusement. "But as much as Chuck here is the greatest, we weren't actually out there giving each other chair dances for shits and giggles. We were practicing."

Chuck nodded enthusiastically, his cheeks tinged a faint pink.

I perked up. "Practicing? For what?"

Chuck grabbed my hand and spun me around, dipping me before swooping in and stealing a kiss.

"For you, of course!" he answered, pressing another soft kiss to my lips.

I locked my arms around his neck and held on, deepening the kiss until we were both panting.

When he finally brought me back upright, I was almost dizzy.

"And you," I turned to Belfast and poked him in the chest, "I saw what you were teaching him. You did this for me?"

His bright green eyes crinkled, and he reached out to tuck my hair behind my ear.

"There's nothing I wouldn't do for you, *a stór*. Come hell or high water. You're home. You're where I belong. I know it here." He tapped his heart, and I stepped into his embrace, holding him tightly to me as a few tears escaped down my cheeks.

"If you guys were practicing for me, does that mean a show is in store sometime soon?" I asked, leaning into Belfast and reaching out to grasp Chuck's hand.

"Oh? Our lady wants a show?" Belfast waggled his eyebrows at me before picking me up and throwing me over his shoulder firefighter-style. I shrieked in protest, but he just laughed and slipped his hand up my skirt, teasing me.

I slapped his ass in protest as he stalked through the kitchen towards the door to the deck. Glitter covered me and I contemplated biting him.

Chuck walked ahead of us and opened the door, ushering us out into the late afternoon heat. This close to the ocean, the sound of the waves and the gulls surrounded us.

Grinning like an asshole, Belfast carefully flipped me over and deposited me in the overstuffed deck chair that had most recently held Chuck and that... dance.

He cupped my chin and kissed me with an intensity that was almost dreamlike. By the time he finally pulled away, I was dazed and thankful I was sitting down.

Freaking Matestone or... whatever this is. I want all of them so bad I literally can't think straight.

Chuck watched us with a smirk on his face. Gone was the insecure, shy man I had first met. This version of Chuck was confident and walked with a little swagger. He moved over to the music and started messing with it. The intro to Shakira's *Hips Don't Lie* piped out of the small bluetooth speaker, and I grinned and sat back to enjoy the show.

I wasn't sure what they had planned, but I had a feeling I was going to be very, very satisfied.

Chuck and Belfast exchanged a smirk, and then they both danced. It was both playful and sensual as they swayed and gyrated to the beat. The progression of the song brought them a step closer to me until I was sandwiched between them. They showed off their impressive bodies to me, moving slowly so I could get a good look.

My pulse raced, and I gripped the edge of the chair to prevent myself from doing something awkward and terrible—like grab them and pull them down into a puppy pile or something. *Down, girl. Oh... what if they went down? Oh gods.*

Belfast was in his element. Now that I had more memories back, I distinctly remembered watching him dance at the Club. He always moved with such grace and sensuality. Everything about him invited you to look and appreciate. He was a beautifully decorated object to be admired. But the way he danced next to me, his brilliant green eyes wild and his smile bright—it was like his carefully practiced mask had dropped just for me.

The emotion in his eyes drew me in and I bit my lip as I watched him. This was the real Belfast, and I had a feeling it had been a very long time since he'd let someone in. I blew him a kiss, and he gave me the sweetest smile and then looked over at Chuck. I followed his gaze and inhaled sharply. Chuck was shaking it to the beat like a freaking pro. Shakira's hips certainly didn't lie, but neither did Chuck's.

If this is how I die, so be it. It was worth it.

Chuck's energy was frenetic, as if the moment might escape him somehow if he didn't dance to his fullest. He gave it his all, and I bopped along with the beat. Neither of them touched me while they danced, and I had a death-grip on the chair's armrest to prevent myself from touching them.

I wanted them and I knew they wanted me, too, but I felt shy. Like, somehow, making the first move acknowledged that this batshit crazy situation was actually real and they, these impossibly beautiful men, were actually fated for me.

The music changed, and before I could blink Belfast had pulled me to my feet. In a flash he was kneeling in front of me and Chuck was standing behind me. Lust burned into my brain and I couldn't think of anything other than the two of them touching me, together. I could feel the evidence of Chuck's arousal pressed up against my back and it felt *impressive*. My hands rested in Belfast's hair, lightly caressing him.

"Our mate is excited to have us here, Belfast," Chuck whispered as he ran his finger down my collarbone, making me shiver.

Belfast grinned at me, and I twitched in anticipation. *Oh my gods, oh my gods, Oh. My. Gods.*

"Chuck, should we show her what we've been practicing?" Belfast asked as he moved his hands slowly up my leg, caressing me in bold, sure strokes.

I nodded my head vigorously. *Yes. Yes, please gods, yes. I want it.*

Chuck laughed quietly and bent down to capture my earlobe in his teeth. He pulled lightly, his hot breath tickling my neck, and I moaned.

"Sweetheart, I need you to do something for us," he whispered to me, in between kisses. Belfast continued stroking me, his fingers getting dangerously close to the tops of my thighs.

"Any-anything." I managed, shakily.

Belfast carefully hiked my skirt up my thighs and leaned forward, blowing gently on my heated skin and causing me to squirm.

The ache between my thighs grew more and more insistent, and my breathing was coming in small pants.

Belfast picked up my right hand and brought it to his lips. He pressed a courtly kiss to the top of my knuckles before slipping each finger into his mouth, one at a time. He sucked gently, swirling his tongue around each digit.

The fire coursing through my veins threatened to morph into a veritable inferno.

I wet my lips with my tongue when he finally returned my hand to my thigh and eased it upwards, towards my aching core.

"We want you to touch yourself, Kalena. Will you pleasure yourself while we dance for you?" Chuck whispered, reaching around me to drag his fingertips lightly across my arms again.

My pulse raced, and my palms were damp. I swallowed hard and managed a slight nod. This was so far outside my comfort zone that I actually didn't quite know what to do.

You are getting the world's sexiest lap dance from two men who are devoted to you. Go with it.

Belfast gave me a brilliant smile and Chuck gyrated slightly against my ass in time with the music, his bulge brushing against me in an intoxicating rhythm.

A sudden sense of power and awareness filled me. I had never been the object of such a powerful desire before. The beat picked up and Belfast looked up at me from between my knees and my shyness dropped away.

Feverish hands roamed over my body, stroking and caressing me - demanding my response, and I gave in.

Wiggling my ass against Chuck, I grabbed the hem of my sundress and pulled it up, stretching to pull it over my head. If they could use stripper moves, so could I, right?

Sunshine hit the exposed skin on my stomach, but the dress caught when I tried to pull it over my head, trapping my arms and face in light yellow fabric.

"Fuck, fuck, fuck!" I howled, flailing, trying to free myself, stepping and bumping into both my beautiful men. *Moon Goddess, just kill me now.*

I tried to pull the dress back down, but a button was caught in my hair and downward movements were excruciatingly painful. I panicked and renewed flailing.

"Sweetheart, hold still," Chuck ordered. His voice was laced with authority and I froze on instinct. Firm hands grabbed my hips and anchored me, pulling me back up against a very hard body. I sighed despite my distress and melted against him.

More hands caressed my chest, tweaking my nipples before working to free me from the evil dress.

They tugged, and I screeched in pain. Chuck dropped a kiss on my shoulder and swayed behind me. Belfast muttered something in Gaelic and I bit my lip so hard it bled a little.

Such a perfect moment. Ruined.

"*A stór*, how much do you want to keep this dress?" Belfast asked, his accent thick and his voice low.

"I hate the fucking thing. It's basically ruined everything. Shred it. Just let me out!" I snapped, fighting back the tears of frustration with limited success.

"Excellent. Hold very, very still, love."

I inhaled and held my breath.

There was a tug and then the sound of ripping fabric. Something cold and metal touched the back of my neck and then I was free. Sunshine streamed down on my flushed face, momentarily blinding me with its brightness.

A few stray tears tracked down my cheeks, but Belfast framed my face with his hands and stepped into me, sandwiching me against Chuck. His thumbs brushed away the stray tears while he studied my face.

"No tears, my love. We're not nearly done."

These men were like a fantasy come to life, and I reached one shaking hand over my thigh and pinched myself. Hard. *Ow.*

Belfast saw the movement and his eyebrow rose.

"Sometimes I can't believe this is actually happening," I whispered before I snaked my arms around his neck and rocked up on my tiptoes. My eyes fluttered shut just as our lips met. His mouth covered mine and my heart danced in excitement, beating along with the music.

Belfast kissed me sweetly, letting me sink into his embrace and take the lead while I got comfortable. Chuck pressed up against my back and kissed my neck as if this were the most normal thing in the world. *Which, I suppose, if I have three mates; it is.*

When I writhed against them both, Belfast smiled into his kiss and carefully withdrew, resting his forehead on mine.

"You are beautiful and I ask myself every day how I got so lucky to have a chance with you."

His words made me tear up with emotion, but before I could respond, he stepped back and carefully spun me around so I was face to face with Chuck.

Chuck smiled at me and tucked my hair behind my ear.

"Hello, sweetheart," he whispered huskily, "I've waited for you for my entire life."

I melted and reached up to kiss him, but he stepped back, grabbing my hand and pulling me along with him.

I let him pull me back to the chair. Gently, he pushed me back onto the cushion and stepped back. His hard length was fully outlined against the tight green shorts and I licked my lips.

We'd play it their way for now, but I needed more. *Soon.*

"Do you remember what you promised?" Chuck asked, standing over my legs. He raised my chin with the tip of his finger and I met his eyes and nodded. Without breaking eye contact, I reached behind me, undid my bra, and eased the straps off my shoulders. His eyes flashed with such potent desire and approval that it took my breath away.

Belfast cued the music again, and Chuck reached with one hand to clutch the back of the chair. At the sound of the beat, he dropped his hips to straddle mine. He hovered over me, barely an inch between us, as he moved slowly over me, gyrating his hips and thrusting. Every sensual movement caused his bulge to rub against me, and I could barely concentrate on anything else.

Belfast was behind us, his hands reaching over the back of the chair to palm my breasts and trail his fingertips down the sensitive sides of my neck.

My entire body erupted in goosebumps when he blew softly along my skin. In an effort to follow directions, possibly for the first time in my life, I reached up to palm my heavy breasts and play with my pebbled nipples. Chuck groaned in approval and wound his fist in my hair, pulling me forward and crushing my lips to his. Our connection was primal and wild and... addicting. I moaned into his mouth, my palm sliding down his chest towards the waistband of those ridiculous shorts. *Is this what a matesbond feels like? Fuck, I'm in serious trouble.*

"Not yet, sweetheart," Chuck whispered against my mouth. I pouted when he pulled away and carefully slid down my body to kneel between my legs.

Belfast came around the side of the chair and knelt down next to Chuck. My breath caught in my throat and my eyes danced between the two of them.

They both grinned, and each took a knee and carefully pushed my legs open.

"You've been slacking, sweetheart," Chuck admonished, sliding his hand up my inner thigh. "I don't see you doing what we asked."

He turned to Belfast and gave him an exaggerated shrug.

"We'll take care of you, *a stór*," Belfast's fingers locked under the waistband of my panties, "Just say the word."

"Word!" I blurted, flushing scarlet red.

Chuck and Belfast both beamed at me and worked in tandem to remove my underwear.

I leaned back in the chair to help them wiggle the fabric down my thighs and then looked down at them expectantly.

A flicker of apprehension coursed through me. "Wait!" I blurted again, "Does this mean we are matesbonded? If we do this?"

Belfast gave me a soft smile and rubbed the top of my

thigh. "No. To accept a matesbond, a ritual must be conducted to seal it. This is only for your pleasure."

I thought for a moment and then spread my legs wider and nodded.

The cords of connection in my chest were burning even brighter, and I pushed all the feelings of lust and desire I had into each of their connections.

Chuck reacted first. His normal baby blue eyes turned a steely grey, and he pulled me forward, gripping my thighs. The slight stubble of his unshaved jaw rasped against my thigh, and I sighed happily.

The first touch of his tongue sent a delicious shock-wave through me, and instinct made me reach down and clutch his hair, holding his head in place.

Every nerve ending in my body was alive and alert. I tried to concentrate and chase my pleasure, but a part of me was scared I was going to shift again. I closed my eyes and scrunched up my face, willing myself to stay in this form.

"Open your eyes, *a stór*," Belfast's voice was husky with desire. "Watch us as we please you."

I cracked open my eyes and saw Chuck moving over slightly, making room for Belfast to dip his head between my thighs as well. They were head to head, working together to worship me.

One of them slipped a finger inside my ready wetness, pushing a second finger in when I rocked my hips against their hand and moaned.

"You are so wet for us, sweetheart," Chuck crooned, looking up at me with a smile on his face.

He curved his fingers and stroked me deeper, making me squirm in pleasure. Belfast sat up and sucked on his finger before carefully rubbing small circles on my sensitive nub. Pleasure shot through me and I gasped.

"That's it, *a stór*. Let yourself go," Belfast encouraged, rubbing me faster. The pressure and sensation built within me and I gasped, rocking my hips against them both, chasing after that elusive release. My hands went to my breasts, and I rolled my nipples between my thumb and finger, pinching each time Chuck thrust his fingers inside me.

"More. I need more," I gasped, arching my back.

Belfast quickly moved his hand away from my clit and licked his fingers, inserting one and then two inside me. *Two men. Two men are fingerbanging me at the same time. Holy Goddess.*

Belfast and Chuck touched foreheads, leaning into each other to maximize the angles for my pleasure.

I was panting, almost ready to lose myself in the stroking, licking and petting. Almost. A part of me was still scared to let go. As much as I wanted, *needed to,* the fear was there. *What if I shifted again?*

Belfast leaned back down to suck on my clit and any thoughts of shifting flew out the window in the face of incredible pleasure.

Heart pounding, body quivering, I teetered on the brink. *Please, Koala. Let me have this.*

"Come for us, sweetheart, just let go," Chuck whispered.

I couldn't take it anymore. I gave in and everything exploded. My climax came in convulsive waves, gushing over their fingers as I clenched and writhed around them. The magic that always lay below my skin swirled into a tempest, sending fiery currents of sensation coursing through me and short circuiting my brain.

Belfast and Chuck anchored me, riding out my release with soft, gentle strokes.

When I had finally come down, I looked down at the two of them and smiled softly.

"I have never come like that before. That was... incredible. And! I didn't shift!"

They turned to each other, eyes shining with satisfaction, and withdrew their fingers from my aching pussy. Chuck moved first, reaching for Belfast and pulling him in for a hug and whispering something in his ear.

A warm feeling flooded through me as I watched them embrace. They were incredibly comfortable with each other for two guys who had just met but, then again. I had just let them fingerbang me to completion, and I hadn't known them all that well either.

Some people open up fast.

They continued their whispered conversation, still holding each other and kneeling between my legs, and I stretched out. Carefully, I pulled my legs up and tucked my feet under my ass in the chair and turned slightly to watch the ocean waves.

I couldn't remember a time when I was more content. All that was missing was Frank. I smiled softly to myself and tugged on his connection to say hi. He would be so pleased when he learned I could orgasm without shifting. Maybe then we could finish what we started the other day.

"Hey, do you think Frank is coming back soon?" I asked, turning back to Chuck and Belfast. My mouth dropped open, and I felt heat rise from my core.

Chuck had looped his hands around Belfast's neck and was leaning in. Belfast pulled the smaller man closer and their lips crashed together in a burning kiss I couldn't look away from. They were perfect together.

My skin prickled again, and I stuffed my fist in my mouth to keep from crying out. Belfast moaned into the kiss and I felt my control slipping. My koala had cooperated for my big moment, but she didn't seem that interested in cooperating for the next one.

Somewhere in the house, a door banged open and heavy footsteps ran towards us. I snagged a bright pink beach towel from the basket next to the chair and tried to wrap myself in it.

The sliding door burst open and a small circle of black flames opened in the center of the deck.

Chuck and Belfast sprang apart just as Frank roared and a tall man in a brightly colored bathrobe stepped out of a portal.

I screamed in pain as my body tried to shift, panting as I tried to fight it.

Chuck and Belfast were standing in a defense position around me, their glitter-covered muscles glinting in the sunlight and the tents in their booty shorts, leaving nothing to the imagination.

Frank looked frantic, and he rushed towards me, scooping me up in his enormous arms and holding me close to him.

I turned to inhale that addicting pine scent of his and my towel slipped.

"Well, this is delightful. You must invite us over more often! Kalena? I'm Bilexphilies and this is Moray, we're here to help you shift." The bathrobe guy walked over to stand behind Frank and offered me his hand.

I reached out to shake it but fur popped up on my arms and I screamed in frustration causing all three of my mates to close in around me.

I looked at Frank tearfully and pressed a small kiss to his lips.

"I didn't shift when I came," I breathed, counting to ten as the pains wracked my body. "It only happened after Chuck and Belfast started making out."

Frank turned to his pod-mates with murder in his eyes, and I put my hand on his chest to calm him.

"I liked it, Frank. They didn't do it for me, they did it for them and I watched and *I liked it.*"

The pain in my chest grew sharper, and I cried out, my knees buckling. Frank caught me and helped me over to the chaise.

The strange pale man who had accompanied the bathrobe guy knelt before me and hovered his hand over my head.

"I am Moray." He said kindly.

"Her animal is dying," he looked up at the others after a long moment, "We have little time."

White hot pain raced through me and my body arched and wrenched, struggling to complete the shift.

The man with the horns had called some sort of smokey magic, and I smelled the acrid scent of sulfur right before my eyes fluttered closed.

"—don't want to die," I whispered before collapsing completely.

Chapter Fifteen
Belfast

My magic flared the second Kalena collapsed in Frank's arms. Golden light flowed through my fingers as I called the whole goddamn rainbow to me and felt the rush of power as it hit me.

The strangers that had portaled in were still hovering over Frank and my mate. I eyed them warily. The smaller, paler one who had announced Kalena's koala was dying radiated an ancient power that reminded me of home. The other one was even older, and the tendrils of his power easily overwhelmed everyone else. His power felt more chaotic—like pure energy with just the slightest hint of darkness.

Either way, these two were clearly powerful and could hold their own.

I shouldered my way into the knot of people hovering over Kalena and glared at the chaotic one, noting the polished horns that poked up just above his hairline.

Demon. Great.

"What did you do to her?" I demanded.

The demon one raised his eyebrow and stared back at

me. "Excuse me? Is this not your mate? Should I not save her," he asked in an acerbic tone.

"Bilexphiles," The smaller one placed a hand on his sleeve and gave me a small smile, "My name is Moray, this is Bill. We mean your mate no harm. Frank brought us the concerns about her shifting and we are here to assist."

A couple of gold coins fell from my cloud of rainbow power, and I picked them up hastily before nodding tightly at the two ancients.

We could use all the help we could get.

The smooth texture of the gold coin in my hand reminded me of the Anam Cara, and a sense of dread flowed through me.

"Her Matestone? How long does it have left?" I asked Chuck and Frank.

Frank looked at me with worry in his eyes, and Chuck scrambled to his feet.

"I don't know, but I'll go get it."

"Bring us a blanket, too," Frank called back, his eyes never leaving our prone mate.

Bill sent another cloud of smokey energy towards Kalena and I saw her cheeks flush pink.

"Matestone? Really? That's most interesting. Another Matestone for Misty Cove." Bill looked at me with a mysterious smile. Reaching up, he pulled a single golden thread out of my magic and held it to his nose and inhaled deeply.

His dark eyes narrowed at me, and he cocked his head.

"What is it they call you here?" he asked, still toying with my golden thread.

I felt sick to my stomach. The last thing any of us needed was someone digging into my background, especially when Kalena was at risk.

"They call me Belfast." I answered shortly, kneeling

down to pat Kalena's hair and press a kiss to her forehead.

"I see," Bill continued, "Well, *Belfast*. Do not think you can hide your true self forever."

An icy chill crept over my body and I gritted my teeth. Chuck saved me from an angry retort when he came sprinting back to the porch, clutching the Matestone and a blanket. Tenderly, he covered our mate with the blanket and then stood and faced Bill and Moray.

"This is the Matestone." he said, opening up his palm.

Bill's eyebrows hit his hairline, and he plucked it carefully from Chuck's hand. "The *Anam Cara* is a Matestone? How delightful."

I cringed but kept silent.

Moray looked over, and his eyes widened. "It's glowing yellow!"

Chuck, Frank, and I exchanged glances, each of us unsure of what to say. Frank spoke first, "So what if it is? Is that bad?"

Moray licked his thin lips and then looked down at our precious mate. "It means she's out of time."

I lost control over my magic for a moment and hard gold coins rained down on all of us, causing Chuck and Frank to fling their bodies over Kalena to protect her.

"What the fuck, Belfast? Get control." Frank growled.

I groaned and concentrated hard, but the gold coins continued to fall.

My mind was racing with everything and it was making me feel slightly seasick. Head in my hands, I staggered over to the chair we had danced with Kalena on and sank into the cushions. The scent of her surrounded me, stirring the memories of what we had done.

The *Anam Cara*... Finding Kalena. Loving her. Building this strange little family. Kissing... Chuck. Watching Kalena suffer.

It was almost too much to hold.

I sensed a presence behind me, and an icy hand rested on my shoulder. The faint scent of sulfur surrounded us, and I shivered in distaste.

"She needs you to control it, Your Highness." Bill whispered in my ear.

My blood ran cold at the casual use of my title. I snapped my head up to look at Bill. I wanted nothing more than to punch that smug expression off his face. Rage warred with worry within me, but I pulled on the golden threads that formed the cloud of my magic, the inner workings of my rainbow. The clatter of coins on the deck slowly stopped, and I could exhale, finally.

"Do not tell them. That is not your information to share," I hissed at Bill before getting up and stalking over to Frank and Chuck.

Moray was sitting cross-legged on the ground and talking animatedly to Frank.

"If the Matestone is running out and her koala is dying, our hands are tied to what we can do. Years of deprivation by magic have divorced her completely from her animal. They are too separate."

Frank let out an anguished roar and Chuck had a steady stream of silent tears dripping down his face.

"Is there anything we can do? Anything at all?" I pleaded with them.

Moray and Bill looked at each other uneasily, and I pounced.

"There is something, isn't there? Well? Tell us, please! Even if it's a long shot we—" I looked at my pod-mates for affirmation, "We want to know."

Chuck nodded wordlessly, and Frank stroked Kalena's arm before standing to his full height and towering over all of us except Bill.

"Whatever we need to do, just save her. Please." The emotion in his voice almost ripped me in two.

Moray hesitated, and then he nodded. "There's an ancient ritual. It basically forges a new connective pathway between Kalena and her koala. It's fallen out of favor because of the difficulty and... abysmal records of success. She's weak and I don't know if she could even complete it as she is now."

Frank paced the length of the deck and Chuck wiped his face and sniffled.

I was frozen in place, my brain working overtime to process what he was saying to me.

I will not lose her. Not when I just found her.

"Is there anything we can do to add to the chances of success?" I asked.

Moray shook his head, but then his eyes lighted on the Matestone.

"If she completed the bonds. Or even one bond. That would give her some more strength."

My heart sank. All of us wanted nothing more than to complete our matesbonds with Kalena, but the rules of the Matestone were extremely clear. She had to choose us and formalize our bond. We couldn't force that bond on her, not even to save her life.

"Can you wake her?" I asked Bill, quietly. He hesitated at my question but nodded his head once. I held up my hand to stop him before turning to the rest of my pod-mates.

"What if.. What if we had Bill wake her and explained the situation to her? I don't know how long she will be awake for, but... it would give her a chance to agree and to verbalize the desire to bond with one of us and complete the ritual. That way, we know what she wants."

Frank nodded, and so did Chuck. "Do it." Chuck

looked at Bill.

I held up my hand again, "Moray, can you explain the ritual first? So we know what we are telling her?"

Moray pursed his lips and then looked down at his feet. "It requires a maelstrom. If she can survive in the center, while the incantation is read, and an offering is made to appease the sea, she could find favor and have her ailment repaired."

Chuck looked pale. "A maelstrom. How… where do we find one? We have nothing like that around here and she can't exactly swim."

"I will create one." Moray said simply, standing to his feet and looking out at the tranquil ocean. "And we can take one of my boats."

Chuck would not be deterred. "YOU will make one? How can you *make* a maelstrom?" he asked suspiciously, moving closer to the smaller man.

Frank extended his arm and stopped him. "He's the Kraken."

Moray whirled around, his navy blue eyes flashing. "Frank." he warned, "You overstep."

Frank raised his hand in apology and then gestured down to Kalena. "There's nothing I wouldn't do to save her. That includes crossing you if I must, my friend."

The tension between them was palpable and Chuck and I stared between them, wide-eyed. Frank squared his stance and lifted his chin in defiance. Moray was flexing his fingers rapidly and muttering under his breath. A steady stream of sea water dripped out of his jacket and I felt the first twinge of alarm.

"You're THE kraken?" Chuck finally asked with awe in his voice. "There is only ever one and you've been here? In Misty Cove? This entire time? Wow!"

Moray stopped muttering to look at Chuck with an

inscrutable expression on his face.

"I am Kraken, yes. I came here for peace and reflection and *privacy*."

Chuck, Frank and I nodded in understanding. "You have your own reasons, I'm sure, and I don't need to know them. I just want my mate back." I said. Moray visibly relaxed a little and Frank backed down.

Motioning to Bill, Moray knelt back down next to Kalena and took her hand in his. "It will have to be the dolphin who bonds with her first. He's the only one of you that could keep her safe in the maelstrom. I cannot guarantee her safety as I will have to concentrate."

Frank growled menacingly and made Chuck jump, but he clapped him on the shoulder. "You save her for us."

Chuck paled but nodded. Bill started muttering a spell that caused all the hair on the back of my neck to rise.

Slowly, Kalena's eyes fluttered open, and she blinked, looking around at all of us in confusion.

"Wha-what happened?" she mumbled.

I leaned forward and cupped her chin. "*A stór*, you must listen to us. You're sick."

Frank grasped her hand and stroked her arm. "It's your koala, love. She's... dying." his voice was thick with emotion and Kalena blinked.

"Oh. Does that, could that mean that my little problem would go away?" she asked, searching our faces for answers.

Frank sucked in a breath, and Chuck pressed a shaking hand to his shoulder to steady him.

"No, sweetheart. You and your koala are bound. If she dies, so do... you. It's the nature of shifters."

Kalena paled and propped herself up on her elbows. "But there's a plan, right? You guys are going to save me from that? Aren't you?"

Chuck looked at Moray and took a deep breath. "There's a plan, but it's dangerous and there's a real possibility it won't work."

I watched Kalena's face while Chuck outlined the ritual step-by-step. She was so brave, nodding along with what Chuck said.

Our fierce mate.

"I can't swim," Kalena wailed when Chuck finished, throwing herself back on the chair in despair.

"Your dolphin mate will keep you afloat in the maelstrom," Moray spoke quietly. Kalena looked at Chuck and then sniffled. "Ok. Let's do it."

We all let out a sigh of relief. Part One complete.

"There's one more thing, sweetheart," Chuck started, a small blush staining his cheeks.

"The Matestone timer is almost up. Moray says you'll have a better chance at surviving the ritual if you have at least one matesbond in place."

All the blood drained from her face and she looked like she was about to faint again. My heart clenched. I knelt before her and beckoned Frank and Chuck to join me.

We each reached out to touch her and her breathing evened out.

"We don't want to rush or pressure you, love." Frank rubbed her knee with one hand and his eyes with the other.

Kalena was silent for several minutes and my heart thundered in my ears. Then, a warmth started in my chest and spread outward, filling me with contentment and love. I turned to Frank and Chuck and they were looking down at their chests in amazement.

Kalena sat back up and smiled at us.

"I've spent the last 36 years believing I would never truly belong. I don't fit in anywhere. Not with witches, not with shifters, not with my family. But this? I actually fit here." She rubbed her finger over the Matestone and then looked up at us with a brilliant smile on her face.

"I still don't fully understand why or how Fate chose me. But I know I can feel each of you in my heart. You each have a distinct glow. It's tangible. I can... feel your emotions and send my own. I don't know how that happened, but... it feels like the start of something, y'know? Something special. I think the matesbonds have already started and, well, I would like to complete them."

"Are you saying what I think you are?" Frank growled, his entire body tense with anticipation.

Her eyes softened, and she reached out to caress his cheek.

"You saved me out in the desert and brought me here. You never hesitate to lend me your strength, and you make me feel safe and cared for. Will you be part of my pod, Frank?" she asked quietly. "Will you protect me forever as my mate?"

I held my breath as Frank vibrated from head to toe. I knew his bear was aching to shift and celebrate, but he controlled himself. With exquisite tenderness, he leaned over her and captured her lips with his. She moaned, pressing herself into him and intensifying their kiss. Happiness radiated through the connection in my chest and I smiled so wide it hurt my face.

Frank finally pulled away and Kalena looked at Chuck with a slightly dazed expression, her lips swollen from kissing Frank.

"And you, Chuck? From the moment we met, you and I connected. You opened yourself up to me with such sweetness and honesty. It makes me feel cherished. Will you join my pod too? Will you connect with me and love me as my mate?" she asked.

Chuck actually climbed up on the chaise and molded her body to his. She threw her leg over his and pulled him closer to her while Chuck peppered her face with kisses and sweet whispers.

Just as quickly as he had hopped up there, Chuck climbed off and Kalena's eyes fell to mine.

"Belfast?" she started

My eyes flew to Bill, and I took a deep breath and interrupted her.

"It's Odhran, actually. Belfast is my stage name, and I understand why you would want to use it, but, I think you should know my actual name."

A slow smile spread across her face, and she crooked her finger at me, calling me forward.

"Odhran," she whispered, "my best friend. The glittering light in my life. You saw me when no one else did, and I could scarcely believe it then. But you make me feel like anything is possible, like we could conquer the world together. Will you be part of my pod? Will you be my best friend and my lover forever as my mate?"

A full body shiver wracked me, followed by an intense wave of happiness when I heard my name on her lips for the first time.

There was nothing I wanted more.

I buried my face in her hair and inhaled her scent. *I was finally home. Family is who you choose, and Kalena and our pod were my true family.*

Someone cleared their throat, and I pulled away reluctantly. Moray looked apologetic and Bill was wiping a tear from the corner of one eye.

Moray wasn't focused on us, but the Matestone that was sitting on the blanket. It was almost out of shine.

"We need to go."

Chapter Sixteen
Chuck

A strange mix of euphoria and fear dogged every step we took as we made our way to the pier and Moray's shop. Our hodge-podge group attracted a fair amount of attention.

Moray and Bill were not the type to be seen in public that often. Frank and Belfast radiated malice to anyone who dared get within three feet of Kalena as they flanked protectively around her and helped move us through the small crowds of people. *My pod. Protecting our mate.* The gossip lines would run for hours at this event. Misty Cove was a supernatural small town, but it was still a small town and people loved getting the dirt on everyone else.

Kalena chose me to walk next to her, and I was almost beside myself with pride. We walked hand in hand and the feel of her soft, warm hand against mine made my heart almost burst with happiness. I could almost forget that we weren't walking in the sun for fun.

Please, Moon Goddess, let this work. Let us save her.

Moray and Bill were muttering behind us in some language that reminded me of the hiss of a snake. Whatever they were saying, it was heated and drawing attention from passersby.

"So, how does it work? How do I.. you know… claim you? Or you claim me? Is it sex or something else? Frank told me it's different for each kind of supe." Kalena spoke up suddenly.

A flush crept down the back of my neck, and I cleared my throat.

"Erm. So, I actually don't know what my dolphin needs to claim you. I didn't grow up with my family pod, so I was never instructed." I confessed, feeling the hot heat of embarrassment cover me. *She's going to regret claiming me now.*

Kalena was silent for a long moment, and my heart thundered in my chest.

"Well, that's kind of perfect considering I don't know the first thing about claiming anything as a shifter, much less what my koala needs. Maybe we just wing it? A lot of magic is about intent. If we get out there and put our energy into our intent, maybe our animals will get on board?"

I smiled tightly at her and nodded. *I hope that will be enough.*

We arrived at Moray's office and the others crowded inside, talking over each other about plans, but I stayed near the door, my heart in my chest.

What if I didn't do it right?

What if the reason my mate dies is that I don't know how to claim her?

Panic seized my throat, and I braced myself against the door frame. An icy cold hand touched my arm, and I nearly jumped out of my skin. Moray appeared next to me, studying me with a thoughtful look on his face.

"You are scared." he said matter-of-factly. I nodded, but couldn't make the words come out.

"Trust your dolphin and let him sing to her. When you're out there. She is your mate and the bonds have already begun. He knows what to do."

As quickly as he appeared, Moray left, melting into the shadows like the mysterious being that he was.

Trust my dolphin. It was all I could do.

"Are you ready?" Belfast called, spying me over at the door and beckoning me closer.

I waved a hand up in acknowledgement and stepped into the room. *Dolphin, don't fail me now. We have to protect our mate.*

THIS WAS ACTUALLY HAPPENING. We were on a boat speeding out to the far side of the Channel Islands. The wind whipped against us furiously and storm clouds gathered in the distance. It was almost as if the ocean knew we were about to ask a favor.

Bill took his leave and disappeared as soon as we piled into the boat, muttering something about hellfire and salt-water not mixing. Moray had shifted as soon as he hit the water and disappeared.

The only evidence that we even had the Kraken on our side was the occasional tentacle that popped up to point us in the right direction. My dolphin was anxious, the urge to shift and find solace in the ocean was strong.

Frank sat in the bow of the boat with a stoic expression on his face. He was fierce and unflappable. I often wished I could be like Frank. Belfast was uncharacteristically quiet, content to sit on the padded bench seat of the whale-watching boat Moray had loaned us. He sipped green tea and made a concerted effort not to look at the waves. Our Leprechaun was prone to seasickness.

Kalena was a flurry of activity, moving around the boat in excitement. She shrieked when the spray hit her and pointed out seabirds and tried to find Moray amongst the waves. It was the cutest thing I had ever seen. She brought joy to our somber party. Even Moray was humoring her, poking up out of the water to wave at her with his tentacles.

She was so full of life and joy… it made it hard to wrap my head around the fact that she was dying.

We sailed for several hours until we reached a small, forbidding rocky island next to a patch of water that was a deep, inky blue. The larger Channel Islands were just specks on the horizon.

Frank expertly navigated our boat to the shore and anchored in the tiny bay. He lowered the inflatable dinghy that would take him and Belfast to shore.

Kalena threw herself into their arms, kissing them and reassuring them that all would be well. I hung back, attempting to give them some privacy, but Belfast pulled me into the group embrace.

"Chuck will protect you," Frank growled, forcing Kalena to look at him. "You must listen to him, my love. Follow his directions. He's a dolphin. The sea is his domain."

The faith my pod-mates had in me to execute this ritual was an honor. An incredibly terrifying honor.

"We will wait for you with whiskey and a bonfire," Belfast added, snapping his fingers and pulling an ancient-looking bottle of Irish whiskey out of thin air or where he kept his stash. Kalena laughed and swiped it from him, opening it to take a swig before handing it back. *Smart girl.*

"Come back to us. Both of you." Belfast looked at

Kalena for a long moment before turning those brilliant green eyes on me. A myriad of confusing feelings rose in me, and I didn't trust myself to speak. I just nodded, pulling my pod-mates into a fierce hug before taking Kalena's hand and stepping back to let them disembark.

We *would* return. This crazy crew was my *family*. A pod that was ordained by Fate herself.

Kalena and I watched until they were safely ashore, and the fire was lit.

Her breathing was a little more labored, and she was extremely pale.

"I guess this is it?" she panted, looking apprehensively over the edge of the boat and into the churning waters. The wind was stiff now, and she shivered a bit.

Moray had assured me she wouldn't be at risk for hypothermia and I had to trust him but, the more I watched her shake and shiver, the more uneasy I felt.

It took considerable effort for the two of us to zip her into the neoprene diving suit that would be her only barrier against the punishing ocean. Muttering under her breath, she practiced the words of her part of the incantation while fidgeting with the Matestone.

The storm around us whipped the salt water into our faces, and I saw a small red light shine from beyond the surf. It was time.

I gulped and exhaled slowly. Pulling Kalena into my arms, I kissed her. Our tongues danced as I poured every complicated emotion I had into that kiss, telling her without words how much she meant to me and how far I would go to make sure we got to see our future through.

When we finally broke apart, I didn't wait or say anything. I just stripped off my t-shirt and shorts and pulled us to the edge of the swimmer's deck. With one hand, I fastened the swimmer's tow belt to Kalena and then we jumped.

My body shifted as soon as I hit the water, separating us for a moment. I swam around her legs, propping her up as she treaded water disjointedly.

She grinned in relief when I surfaced and reached out to touch my smooth skin. I preened for her and clicked, making her laugh in delight. Gently, I picked up the tow rope, and she hooked it around my body like we had practiced.

My dolphin hummed in excitement, loving the touch of our mate.

She held onto my dorsal fin and gave me a thumbs up.

I flew through the waves, the icy water invigorating me. The pod and I had discussed this at length and we decided that speed would be the highest priority and Kalena would tap three times on my fin to let me know if she needed a break.

The further we got from the boat, the rougher the surf was. I heard her sputter as the waves crashed over her but she held on tightly. *Just a little further, sweetheart.*

Moray swam up next to me and grabbed the end of the tow rope. He pulled us even faster through the water, cutting through the waves with military precision.

I knew we were in the right place when we crossed into a patch of water that was perfectly still.

The storm raged all around us but here, in this circle of deep, inky blue - it was calm.

Kalena slowly released her death-grip on my fin and slid off me, letting the buoyancy of the swimmer's belt hold her up in the water. Her hands shook as she undid the rope wrapped around me.

Moray's fearsome blue eye peeked up at us from just under the water, checking in.

He pushed us towards the center of the circle, and Kalena squeaked in surprise. Her face was wan and her movements sluggish.

As soon as we were in the center, I shifted back to human form and took Kalena in my arms, easily supporting us both.

"Are you ready, sweetheart?" I whispered in her ear.

"Everything hurts, Chuck. I - can't even feel my magic anymore." she said faintly.

My dolphin was frantic with worry and I held her closer, bitterly resenting the Orcas that had decimated my birth-pod, denying me the crucial knowledge that would allow me to claim her and share my strength with her.

I took both her hands and stared deep into her eyes. Kalena had told me intention was half the battle. I had intention in spades. This woman was my everything.

"I claim you as my mate, Kalena Montague. From this day forward for the rest of our lives. I promise to love you, to care for you, and to live with you in our pod."

Her eyes were wet with unshed tears - or possibly ocean spray - and she clutched me tightly.

"I accept your claim. I claim you as my mate as well. To love, to care for, and to live with as Fate intended." she whispered, her words slurring slightly.

We treaded water, holding each other, and waited.

But nothing happened.

The storm still raged around us, battering the invisible barrier that kept this space calm and sacred. I didn't know what I was expecting, but I thought I would at least feel something.

Oh gods, what if Fate never meant her for me. What if this is all a giant cosmic mistake?

My dolphin was doing flips in my chest, trying to get my attention, but I was too worked up to listen.

Frank had said bears need to bite their mate in order to complete their bond. It always happened during sex, right at climax. He hadn't shared any other details, and it was a bit late to ask now. *Shit.*

If that were true for dolphins too, we were bang out of luck.

Her head fell forward slightly, and she looked like she was minutes away from collapsing.

"It couldn't hurt," I muttered to myself.

"Sweetheart, I think I have to bite you to claim you?" I said, raising my voice to be heard over the howls of the wind. She nodded, and I unzipped the top of her neoprene suit.

This better work.

My dolphin was zooming around my senses, making me feel like I was being minorly electrocuted.

I found the soft spot on her collarbone and brushed it with my lips, softly at first.

When she moaned, I struck.

"I claim you as my mate," I whispered fiercely and sank my teeth into the soft spot.

Her back arched, and she cried out. I pulled her even closer to me and withdrew my teeth, pressing my lips gently to her forehead.

Universe. Moon Goddess. Please. I claim her. I claim her as my mate. I claim her here forever and always.

But nothing happened.

Moray hovered in the background, slowly swimming the perimeter of the ritual spot and drawing the current to him to begin the maelstrom. We were on our own. The ritual had begun.

"Do I - I bite you?" Kalena managed. Her lips were slightly blue, and I panicked.

Quickly, I presented my neck to her, and she dropped

her head onto my shoulder. Her tongue darted out and licked the salt off my skin. She pressed her lips against my shoulder and sank her sharp little teeth into me.

"My mate," she whispered before collapsing against me and her eyes fluttered closed.

My dolphin chose that moment to break free and force my shift. I swallowed a mouthful of water when he took charge, plunging me deep under the surface and zooming towards the bottom of the sea.

I watched helplessly from beneath the surface as Kalena fell backwards, floating listlessly on the water. All alone.

The current of the maelstrom and my dolphin fought against me, driving me downward, towards the edge and away from my mate.

Flashes of green passed me as Moray continued to swim the perimeter, whipping the peaceful water into a furious whirlpool that I was helpless to stop.

I had failed.

I watched in horror as the swirling water reached Kalena and sucked her under.

Flailing against the current, I cried out - my heart breaking in a billion pieces when I lost sight of her.

The current dragged me deeper and deeper when I suddenly remembered Moray's words.

Trust your dolphin. Let him sing.

And there, floating in the maelstrom, I did.

The love for my mate, the pain of potentially losing her, the soul-crushing anguish of failing her poured out of me as my dolphin sang.

Chapter Seventeen
Kalena

Drowning was a very peculiar experience. One minute, I was floating on the surface and semi-aware of everything that was happening around me. Chuck was next to me. Sweet, sweet Chuck.

He was saying the most magical things to me. Claiming me as his. It was beautiful and romantic and everything I wanted. He was my mate.

Then, the next minute, he was gone. Pulled underwater and away from me. He slipped under the surface and just... disappeared.

I floated there for a moment and listened to the rumblings of the water around me and hoped he would return.

But he didn't.

I was alone and so very exhausted.

The current was seductive, whirling faster and faster. It beckoned all in its path to join it. The power of the maelstrom pushed down on the very surface of the water and bent it to its will.

Who was I to fight it? I was nothing. A broken shifter and a mediocre witch.

I smiled when I felt the first tug downward. It was soft, like a lover's caress - promising pleasure and the world if only I gave in.

Part of me wished I could fight it. The faces of Frank and Belfast and Chuck flashed through my mind and my heart stuttered.

But the water tugged at me again, seductive and persuasive. We both knew the truth. I could give in or I could fight, but either way - the ocean would win.

It wasn't your fault. I loved you. All of you. I whispered, praying to the Moon Goddess that my mates would hear it in their hearts and know the truth.

Then I gave in. The next time the water lapped at me, I let it.

As if sensing my surrender, the water gently pulled me down and down.

I sank.

I didn't have the strength to fight it, even if I wanted to.

The colors under the surface were surprising. I watched as a steady, techno-color stream of colors swirled around me. My lungs burned, but I didn't fight to the surface.

My vision blurred, and I clenched on the cords in my heart connecting me to my mates. It wouldn't be much longer.

A strange song echoed in my ears as I felt my life force seeping out of me. It was eerie and beautiful all at once. The notes wrapped around me like a blanket, caressing my skin and protecting me. Warmth radiated out from my core and took the pain away. I felt alert and awake. My lungs no longer burned. I inhaled through my nose and marveled at the flood of oxygen that hit my lungs.

Am I dead? What is this?

An explosion of emotion hit me in the chest, and I gasped, folding over myself. The current carried me even further, but I was filled with strength and I fought it. Propelling myself forward, I swam with the water, spiraling - desperate to get to whoever was singing the song.

Mate. The inner voice in my mind was sure. I felt something stir in my chest and I redoubled my efforts.

Mate. Must find mate.

The water was moving so fast; it was like a blur. Momentum carried me forward deeper through the spiral, and I could only float along and ride the current. With each spiral, the song grew stronger and stronger and my heart cried out at the influx of pain from the singer.

I'm coming. Please don't stop. I'm coming.

The light from the surface was no longer visible. It was getting steadily darker, and I worried again. *Surely, this has to end at some point?*

A flash of grey-blue below me caught my eye and my heart started racing. A single, solitary dolphin was swimming in place in the direct center of the spiral.

MATE. The voice in my head was more insistent. I listened harder, grabbing onto the sound and following it as it pulled me closer.

At the next pass, I lunged out of the current and threw myself into the center of the maelstrom, sinking rapidly towards my mate.

The water tried to intervene. To prevent me from reaching my mate. But I would not be deterred. At long last, I reached out and dragged my fingertips along the back of the singing dolphin, hooking my hands around his dorsal fin and swinging around to face him. When I touched him, something clicked into place and I felt a jolt of euphoria.

He stared at me for a moment, as if he could hardly believe I was real.

Before my eyes, he shifted, and my mate was back. His light blonde hair floated all around us in the water, and his baby blue eyes sparkled in the dim light.

We lunged for each other at the same time and laughed when the current knocked us together.

His brawny arms held me in place, anchoring me to him. I looked up at him with wonder and love in my eyes.

"I thought I lost you," He said hoarsely.

"Forever, my mate. You have me, *forever*," I promised him, tilting my lips up to meet his.

He kissed away all the fear, the doubt, and the insecurity. In that moment, nothing else mattered but my mate. We floated, our arms locked around each other, oblivious to the inky darkness of the ocean deep or the raging maelstrom around us.

Pain caused us to break apart. The little voice that had so clearly identified my mate was fading and taking with it my strength.

"The ritual!" Chuck cried out, gripping my hand tightly and turning us so we faced the many layers of swirling water.

Together, we said the words as we rehearsed and concentrated on sending our intent into the water.

A steady stream of bubbles floated up from our feet, and I looked down nervously. Moray had said something about a fearsome creature that lived in the deep that sometimes answered these calls when the other sea gods were busy. He had said it so casually then that I had thought he was joking, but now I wasn't so sure.

A rumbling from below shook us, vibrating through the water. I buried my face in Chuck's chest and tried to control my breathing.

Chuck wrapped his arms around me protectively, and we waited for Fate to give us our answer.

"Ahem, excuse me. Hi. Can I help you?" A nasally sounding voice rose from the depths and I chanced a look.

Tiny, saucer-shaped blue eyes blinked slowly at me and I did a double take.

A small, bright red squid was floating in front of our faces, and he looked annoyed.

"Uh," I turned to Chuck for help, but he just shrugged.

"Moray sent us?" I tried, hoping the fear of the Kraken would prevent this small-but-scary creature from harming us.

"Moray? He got out of the game years ago. Gave up his crown and everything." he spat out, flaring his arms out in disgust. I stared. They were all webbed together like an umbrella. A strange squid umbrella.

"She speaks the truth." Chuck started, "She was born to a witch and a shifter. Magic has damaged her shifter side to where she is dying. Our friend, Moray, gave us this ritual in hopes we might find favor from the sea gods."

The squid deflated a bit at that and made a strange whistling noise while it swam in a lazy circle around them.

"You got the payment?" he asked finally.

Chuck nodded and pulled an emerald necklace and a handful of Belfast's Leprechaun gold out of the special pocket attached to my suit.

The squid swam over and looked it over with a bored expression.

"Eh, emeralds aren't my color. And what the hell do you think I need gold for? Have you seen me? Does it look like I get to the surface very often? No. I do not. What else you got?"

I giggled. The little squid was so tiny, probably not even 6 inches long, and yet so terrifying.

"What can we call you?" I asked when he turned those glowing blue eyes on me.

He puffed up and flared his weird web-legs again.

"I am the Emissary of the Channel Depths, Second Secretary to the Sea Lord Poseidon, and last remaining member of the House Vampyroteuthis Infernalis."

I blinked, and he deflated again.

"You may call me Neil."

"Right, Neil. My mate here left out the important bit to our plea. I know you must be a very busy, very important... Emissary, but I must plead with you for your patience in hearing me out." I turned my attention to him and he bobbed in the water, presumably a sign for me to carry on.

Digging in the zippered pocket in the front of my wetsuit, I pulled out the Matestone. The glow was almost gone completely, but it still shone in the dim and I said a small prayer of thankfulness to it for leading me to my mates.

"Do you know what this is, Neil?" I asked, holding it out so he could get a good look.

His big blue eyes bugged out, and he floated closer to my outstretched arm. Chuck tapped my shoulder with a questioning look, but I ignored him, focusing all my attention on the strangely pretentious squid who held the key to my future.

"The *Anam Cara*. I'm not stupid, girlie. I get out every now and again. That's a priceless Fae artifact, that is."

I smiled and closed my fist over it. "It is. But that's not all it is. It's also a Matestone. Fate used it to lead me to my mates, my pod. We've known each other only a short time, and yet they mean everything to me. Will you please, in all of your power and influence, help me so I can fulfill what Fate intended and just... I don't know... be happy for once in my life? Know what it's like to be accepted and loved for who I am?"

Neil swam around us in circles for a few moments before zooming in close to my face.

"The magic you ask for comes with a price. In order to heal you, I must reconnect your animal spirit with your human spirit. I have to channel the ancient powers of the sea. It gives me a wicked headache for days and it will not be pleasant for you." Neil warned.

"The cost is *Anam Cara*." he flared his web again, and I felt nervous.

"I guess, if Fate saw fit to give this to me, she knew I would need it." I intoned.

Neil flared his webbed tentacles again and swam an arms-length away from me.

"You have a deal, Neil." I whispered and let the coin fall from my hand.

Neil swooped in and captured it, cackling with glee.

"Excellent. Close your eyes and *do not* open them until I tell you." he ordered, the nasal quality of his voice suddenly gone and replaced with a deep, husky tone.

I closed my eyes, gripped Chuck's hand tightly, and prayed to the Moon Goddess that I made the right choice.

At first, nothing happened, and I relaxed a bit.

Then, all at once, my entire skin exploded in sensation. I threw my head back in a wordless scream as my body arched and contorted. It took all my concentration to keep my eyes shut as Neil had instructed. Fire burned through my chest and I could almost follow its path. It was burning me from the inside out, purifying the old pathways that were scarred by magic and chasing the last bits of malevolent spells out of my body.

My bones twisted and flexed until the pain was so great that I wanted to quit and give up.

I opened my mouth to beg mercy from Neil when I felt a new stirring in my chest. It felt… distantly familiar.

Hello, Kalena.

My koala was alive, and this time, she could speak to me.

"Wakey wakey," Neil called in my ear, "Open your eyes and let's see if we succeeded."

My eyelids felt glued to my face, but I pried them open and looked around, examining my hands and feet for any obvious signs of koala.

Chuck looked pale and completely horrified.

"I can feel her. My koala." I tapped my chest and smiled in relief.

We did it.

"Well, if that's all you needed. I'll be going." Neil chirped, diving back down into the deep. The rumbling started again, and I stared at Chuck in wonder.

"It worked!" I cried, flinging my arms around his neck.

Chuck twirled me around and then froze.

"Oh, motherfu-" he swore, shifting to his dolphin form effortlessly and grabbing ahold of me.

I held on for dear life as we rocketed up through the center of the maelstrom. The rumbling followed us, almost deafening as the surrounding water sloshed and shook.

"What's happening?" I yelled as Chuck strained to pull us up and up.

"Maelstrom is collapsing. Neil closed it when he went back down. He didn't wait for us to surface. The entire ocean is about to crash down on us."

"Moray!" I screamed as the pressure from the ocean bore down on us. I kicked my feet, trying to help Chuck propel us forward. The higher we went, the harder it was for me to help. Extreme exhaustion weighed me down, and it was a struggle to even keep my eyes open.

Frank and Belfast flashed into my mind, and I pulled at their connections, desperately hoping for strength. I got enough of a boost to drive us forward another 20 feet before I drained completely.

Chuck gripped my arm with his teeth and pulled me foot by foot. As much as I wanted to help, I felt frozen. My koala was telling me how tired she was, and my body refused to ignore her.

I did not just go through all that only to die on the way back up. I have two more mates and a happily ever after to claim, damnit.

Painstakingly, I paddled with my palm and tried to move us forward. My vision was spotty and everything hurt, but I had to get home to my pod.

A flurry of green scales interrupted my vision, and a long, serpentine arm carefully wrapped around me. I shouted for Chuck, but when I looked; he was caught too.

Moray.

We raced through the water, the rays of sunshine growing ever closer.

I breathed a sigh of relief when we finally broke the surface, but Moray didn't let us go. He carefully held us above the surface enough so I could breathe and raced towards the shore.

The ocean spray distorted my vision, but I could see the flickering light of a bonfire in the distance. *My mates.*

My koala bellowed in my chest, startling me with her vociferous nature.

Moray came to a screeching stop about 10 feet offshore and I felt his long arm lean back and then I was flying towards the beach…. and the rocks.

I heard a yell, and then a flash of golden light blinded me. I thudded to a stop in the sparkly, golden arms of Belfast.

"Welcome home, *a stór*," he kissed me on the nose and

waded through the surf towards a very agitated looking Frank.

"Where's Chuck?" I craned my neck, looking behind Belfast to find my beloved dolphin. A shock of white-blonde hair bobbed in the waves and a supreme sense of satisfaction ran through me.

My pod was home.

Frank met us in the water and practically wrestled me out of Belfast's arms.

"I am never letting you go again." He growled in my ear and stomped up the beach.

My koala was bellowing again, and I felt antsy. The prickly feeling started on my skin and I held my breath.

Frank froze and put me down on the sand gently. I braced for the pain, but it never came. Instead, my equilibrium flipped, and I felt extremely dizzy. And then... it was over.

Whoa. Head rush. I'll have to ask Moray how to get a thank you note to Neil.

When I sat back up, everything felt... off. My vision was kind of blurry and I tried to focus.

"Kalena?!" A thundering voice echoed in my head and I screamed, slapping my hands out to get away from whatever made that horrifically loud noise.

Except it wasn't a scream... it was a squeaky bellow and my hands weren't human anymore. They were claws. *Koala claws.*

I had finally shifted. Whoa.

My nose twitched, and I could smell *everything.* The musky predator smell of Frank, the sharp smokey smell of the campfire, the salt spray from the ocean... it all invaded my sensitive nose. The sand felt weird under my paws and there were too many people around me. Someone tried to touch me and I swiped at them, bellowing my rage.

I felt... wild and free. Truly, wonderfully *free*. A kinship with my koala grew in my chest and she demanded I answer her call to the wild.

Ignoring the sounds of the people around me, I trotted off towards the interior of the island. When I felt them follow me, I picked up speed, flying down the beach as fast as my little furry legs could take me.

In the back of my mind I heard three separate voices calling out to me, pleading with me to stop and wait, but I ignored them and ran faster. My sharp claws helped me fly to the top of a tree, and I sat at the top and surveyed my new kingdom.

I was at the top of the world, and I never wanted to leave.

Chapter Eighteen
Kalena

S omething was crawling on me. It tickled at first, like a
tentative skitter across my foot. I almost brushed it off
and snuggled back down to sleep but then it was back.
Sharp, tiny feet poking into my skin and moving up my
calf.

I flailed and kicked my leg out violently to disturb the
intruder and collided with something hard and warm.

"*Mother. Loving. Moon. Goddess!*" someone shouted, and I
startled, flailing again and driving my elbows into another
warm, hard thing.

Hands reached out to steady me and three distinct
voices called out soothing things, petting my hair, my skin
and holding me.

I was surrounded by men. My men.

I turned on my side and was promptly pulled up
against a very hard body, his morning glory poking me in
the back. Directly across from me was a bare chest that
glimmered slightly in the early morning light. Glancing
down at my feet, I saw white-blonde hair and a goofy grin
looking back at me.

Mates.

My heart rate slowed, and I inhaled deeply.

We were sprawled out on the beach. The sun was just peeking up over the horizon, streaks of pink and grey lighting the sky. Several small, red crabs scurried along the waterline in search of breakfast and the gentle call of the seagull echoed through the trees.

If Chuck was down by my feet and Belfast was in front of me, that meant Frank had hold of me. I wiggled against his morning wood and giggled when he growled in my ear and nuzzled my neck with his stubble. *There are worse ways to wake up.*

Belfast grinned at me.

"*A stór*, you sure know how to wake a man up!" he teased, leaning over to press a sweet kiss to my lips. The warmth of his body seeped into me and I looped my hands around his neck to draw him closer, squishing myself between his body and Frank's.

Mine.

A possessive growl started in my chest, and desire pooled between my thighs.

Claim your mates.

I ground harder against Frank and moaned when Belfast dipped his head to take one of my nipples in his mouth.

Vaguely, I realized I was naked, and I couldn't remember why. But as soon as the thought came to me, I banished it. The only thing I wanted, the only thing I needed, was them. All of them.

The ache between my thighs was growing more insistent, and I was desperate for their hands on me.

"Chuck," I called out raggedly while Frank and Belfast slowly worked their magic on me. "Chuck, I need you, too."

Footsteps shuffled around us and I looked up to see

Chuck leaning down over me. He had moved to my head and propped up on his elbows.

I wet my lips with my tongue and he swooped in, stealing a kiss while his pod-mates drove me higher and higher.

"You are mine." I said fiercely, looking at each of them turning awkwardly in the sand to look at Frank. "*Mine.*"

My instinct was to mark them. To claim them as mine.

The wildness I remembered from last night came roaring back and I felt the primal pull of energy between the four of us.

Belfast stroked me gently, his fingertips caressing me as he dropped feather-light kisses on my body. It was romantic. Soft. Gentle. All the elements of the perfect early morning beach seduction.

Except... I didn't want to be gentle.

I had gone to the actual depths of the ocean just so I could come back for these men.

I wanted to claim them. Rough, demanding, primal. I wanted the wildness to flow through us as we moved together, bodies slick with sweat and desire.

And then? When they were on the cusp of losing themselves, crashing their climax into me? I wanted to bite them.

I rolled onto my stomach and pushed up on the soft sand. Standing over them while they lounged on the sand beneath me was a powerful feeling. I took a moment to examine my beautiful mates.

Belfast laid on his back, his golden skin shimmering against the white sand beach. He moved one hand behind his head and stroked his long, thick cock with the other.

My mouth salivated at the sight. I needed to taste him.

Frank sat up and leaned against the tree that was giving us shade. Scars and tattoos decorated his arms, and a sprinkling of dark hair covered his chest. My fingers twitched with the desire to touch him. When my eyes dropped to his swollen cock, I gulped. *Magnificent.*

Chuck smirked at me when I turned to examine him. He was standing, his arms hanging loosely at his side. He had a sleek, powerful build with long, sensitive fingers. I shuddered in pleasure at the memory of those fingers buried deep inside me. His dick pulsed under my gaze and I wanted nothing more than to reach out and stroke him.

These were my mates.

I stepped forward and straddled Belfast, motioning for Chuck and Frank to kneel on either side of Belfast's head.

Dropping to my knees, I rubbed my aching pussy against Belfast's cock and moaned in pleasure. I leaned forward and captured his mouth with mine, our tongues dancing as I rubbed against him, skin to skin.

When he moaned in my mouth, I popped my hips forward and sank down on him, sheathing his entire length in one thrust.

I shuddered as my body adjusted to his size before sitting up, rolling my hips and rocking against him.

Belfast's green eyes flashed with desire as he brought his palms up to anchor my hips, urging me to ride him faster and faster.

My breath came in short pants and I quickened our pace, letting instinct take over.

Chuck and Frank watched us hungrily, their hands fisted around their cocks. I beckoned Frank closer, his kneeling height put his dick just under my face. Every inch of me lit up, demanding I claim them all.

When I reached out and stroked him, he growled, pushing his dick into my hand and matching my pace. This feeling was intoxicating and I couldn't get enough.

I dipped my head and took him in my mouth, bobbing my head in time with each roll of my hips on Belfast.

Sensation exploded around me and my eyes threatened to roll in the back of my head when Chuck leaned forward and captured one of my nipples in his teeth. Together, the three of them stroked me from ember to inferno, until coherent thoughts left my mind and all that was left was feeling.

I felt primal, powerful and, most of all, deeply cherished.

Belfast grunted, and his eyes were glossy in concentration. His body tensed and I let go of Frank and Chuck to lean forward and press my lips against his neck. As he came, I bit down and felt him buck underneath me. My release followed as I felt our connection strengthen. The golden light connected us and flowed through me until I exhaled shakily.

Holy shit.

Eyes wild, I crawled off Belfast, kissing him deeply before scrambling to my feet.

Frank stalked towards me, his eyes dark with desire. He pulled me up against his chest and slanted his mouth over mine, hot and demanding. A hum of satisfaction escaped my lips as he ground his hips into mine.

Spreading my palm against his chest, I toyed with chest hair, running my fingers through it and tracing the lines of a jagged scar before shoving him back hard.

Before he could say a word, I dropped to my knees, spreading out on all fours. His hand knotted in my hair and lined my face up with his dick. I teased him, swirling my tongue around the tip and taking him in shallow strokes before he pulled harder, demanding what he needed.

My entire body tingled with his touch. The sharpness

of the pain in my head combined with the intoxicating power of claiming was enough to drive me over the edge.

Chuck kneeled between my spread legs and pushed me forward, gagging me on Frank's cock while his hands traced the contours of my body.

I was in heaven, and my back arched in response to his touch.

I moved my head up and down, taking as much as I could of Frank while Chuck's swirling fingers spread me wide. I writhed against them both, the pleasure building in me.

Frank's breathing was rapid and his hands were tangled in my hair, driving me forward harder and harder.

I met him stroke for stroke. Tracing his thick veins with my tongue, and forcing my throat to open wider for him, taking him deeper.

As Frank hit the back of my throat, I felt Chuck tease my opening, his blunt tip rubbing against me but not yet entering.

The sensation was maddening. I rocked my hips back, sliding onto him before Frank pulled me back onto his dick.

Back and forth, they used me. Frank fucking my mouth while Chuck thrust into me from behind, clasping my hips hard against him. I had never felt more alive.

When I felt Frank's balls tighten, a raw, rippling wave crashed over me from head to toe. He found his climax with a roar, spilling down my throat. I swallowed it all, licking him clean as the waves crashed through his body. I sank back on Chuck, withdrawing from Frank completely and tilting my head to place my lips on the sensitive part of his inner thigh.

"Mine." I whispered before sinking my teeth into him.

He roared again and the connection between us pulsed to life.

Chuck thrust into me harder and I rocked against him, my hands coming up to palm my breasts. Strong hands encircled my waist, pulling me off of him for a moment and flipping me on my back. Before I could pout or protest his absence, he was back. He pinned my arms above my head and pushed my knees up, wedging himself between my thighs. I was aching for him, throbbing with need when the thick head of his cock drove into me.

Frank and Belfast flanked us, each of them stroking my side - teasing my breasts and kissing me while Chuck pounded into me.

My muscles tensed, and a wave of pleasure crested over me. He covered my mouth with his, swallowing every whimper as we came in mutual surrender.

Chest heaving, I pulled away from his kiss and found his shoulder.

"Mine."

The moment I bit him, the bond we had created in the ocean depths heated and I felt the hum of all my bonds snapping into place. My mates were claimed. It was official. We were a pod. *Do we need a pod name?*

The four of us collapsed in a heap. Our bodies were spent but our spirits were bright and, for the first time in my life, I felt like everything was going to be ok.

WE DOZED NAKED in the sun, waking only to fall into each other's arms repeatedly. I had never felt this content. My mates loved me with ferocious passion and exquisite tenderness until I couldn't see straight.

Sated and slightly sore, I finally dragged myself up

from our snuggle pile and pulled a sarong and swimsuit from Frank's bag.

Telling time via sunshine was not a life skill I possessed, but an evening spent negotiating my freedom with a sea creature, exploring the island as a Koala, and fucking my mates 100 different ways from Sunday made me hungry.

Frank had packed little for breakfast, and our bonfire was down to glowing embers. I munched on a protein bar and watched the waves, contentment sinking into my bones. The only thing missing was the little gold coin I had grown so fond of. I caught myself looking for it more than once and had to remind myself that it had served its purpose and given me the freedom I had now.

Thank you, Fate. For trusting me.

If there was a way to freeze this feeling, bottle it to keep it forever, I wanted to know.

My men slept, arms and legs tangled around each other, and their soft gentle snores warmed my heart. For my first morning as a mated woman with her very own pod, this was turning out pretty damn well.

By the time I had finished my little breakfast, my men were stirring.

"*A stór*," Belfast called sleepily from his snuggled spot between Frank and Chuck, "Come join us! And bring the *Anam Cara* with you. I want to tell you the story of my people and what the *Anam Cara* means to us."

I froze, and ice crowded my veins. There hadn't been time to tell the rest of the pod everything that had happened during the ritual. *Oh shit. Oh shit. Oh. SHIT.*

I panicked and turned away from him, my arms wrapped tightly around me.

I walked until my toes hit the water's edge and I stood there, staring out at the endless blue ocean. Belfast called for me again, but I was frozen in place by guilt.

The Anam Cara was priceless to his people, and I just… traded it without a thought.

"*A stór*, what's wrong?" Belfast asked, coming up behind me to wrap me in his warm arms.

I shrugged him off, biting my lip as the guilt piled on.

"What does that mean? That name you keep calling me? *A stór*?" I demanded, tears threatening to spill down my cheeks.

"It means 'my treasure'," he said quietly, "You're my treasure, Kalena."

My heart beat wildly, and I turned to face him, misery and guilt written all over my face. I did not know how to tell him it was gone.

"I don't have it. I… traded it during the ritual." I admitted, observing his face.

He stepped back as if he had been slapped, and my heart broke.

"You-you gave it away?" He asked hoarsely.

I bit my lip and inclined my head. "It's the only thing Neil would accept to heal my koala."

I reached out to him, desperate for contact and reassurance that he wouldn't hate me, but he stepped back, just out of reach. His face was masked in shock.

"It's gone. It's really gone." he whispered to himself.

I turned away from him to wipe my tears and when I turned back; he was jogging ahead of me on the beach.

My heart shattered into pieces.

I moved to follow him and beg his forgiveness, but a rose-gold flash of light split the sky and three men dropped out of a portal directly in front of him.

I watched, frozen in horror, as Belfast fought the attackers off. Anxiety and fear bubbled to the surface, pinning me in place.

The scream I had been holding back finally made it to

the surface when one man took a bat and cracked Belfast over the head with it. His beautiful, shimmery gold body went limp and the three men tugged him into the rose gold portal.

My feet pounded down the sand as I ran towards him, but it was too late.

Frank and Chuck were close behind me, catching me when I fell to my knees on the soft sand.

I traded the *Anam Cara* away to save my skin, and the next morning someone kidnapped my mate?

It couldn't be a coincidence. Was this my fault?

I turned to Chuck and Frank with a fierce expression on my face.

"We will get him back. Chuck - get me Moray and Bill. I think we need to make a trip to Faery."

I walked back towards our camp, and my toe caught on something hard in the sand. Staring back at me in the sand was a burnished gold coin.

The *Anam Cara* had returned.

Chapter Nineteen
Belfast

My mind was overloaded with emotions when I wandered down the beach. Leaving Kalena there was a dick move, but I couldn't process what she had told me.

The *Anam Cara* was gone.

Traded... for the life of a shifter-witch. Specifically, the shifter-witch who was also my mate.

I would have traded it a thousand times if it meant that Kalena was safe, happy and healthy. There was *nothing* more valuable to me than her.

Yet, losing the artifact - that little piece of my heritage that connected me to Tír na nÓg was painful. I had hoped that I could broker a deal with it. A way to come home and visit my sister and introduce her to my mate and my pod. But now that avenue was closed to me.

I was so lost in my thoughts that I didn't see the portal until it was too late. My emotions churned inside me and Glen, my father's right-hand man, got in two quick punches before I could even respond.

By then, it was too late. I landed a few punches, but the momentum was on the side of my attackers.

Glen, Garrett, and Georgie — the three dickheads my father kept around as muscle, had already overpowered me and forced me into the transport, snatching me right off the beach.

"Your father wishes to speak with you on a matter of great importance, Your Highness," Glen sneered, right before he hit me over the head with his bully bat.

The last thing I saw was Kalena frantically running towards me, with Frank and Chuck closing in behind her. *My pod.*

I bared my teeth at my captors and shook off their hands, but it was too late. The portal whirled me away to Leprechaun Hill.

I committed Kalena's face to my memory and set my sights on the current problem. *My father wants to play power-games? He was about to get more than he bargained for. No one fucks with my mate and my pod. Not even a King.*

WE LANDED in the entryway of the Summer Palace, and I took in a sharp breath as I looked around. My old home had scarcely changed in the 150 years it had been since I last laid foot here. Glen and Garrett flanked me and prodded at me to move me along while Georgie ran ahead to alert the rest of the Palace staff of our arrival.

As soon as Georgie disappeared around the corner, I took advantage of our momentary solitude. One quick jab of my elbow to Glen's throat released his hands from my person. I smiled grimly when he fell back, wheezing. *Don't touch the dancers, asshole!*

Garrett gave me a wide berth as we eyed each other. I was in a precarious position and either way, I would have to acknowledge the gilded elephant in the room.

When he took me by force and dragged me here, my father forced me to acknowledge an uncomfortable truth. Here, I was no longer Belfast.

The freedom I had enjoyed was no longer relevant.

Disgraced or not, the mantle of who I really was fell onto my shoulders, whether or not I liked it.

My father in all his sadistic glory had forced me back to the life I had sworn to leave behind forever, albeit temporarily.

Crown Prince Odhran, Guardian of the Gold and Heir to Leprechaun Hill.

Even the name made my skin itch. But you don't grow up in the Summer Palace without knowing how the politics worked.

I cracked my neck and sighed heavily. If this was who I was required to be to get back to Kalena and the rest of my pod, so be it. *Game. On. Daddy-O.*

I closed my eyes and sank into the persona I had been groomed to adopt since I was an infant. Cold. Unyielding. *Royal.* A flash of my magic had me clothed in a well-fitted suit fit for a prince.

"Well? What are you waiting for? Take me to my father before I lose my patience with you, too." I snapped at Garrett, stepping over Glen who had collapsed on the floor still wheezing.

There was no point in waiting for a reply. Royalty never waited for inferiors. We ordered and expected compliance.

I marched down the hallway without waiting for him, eyeballing the decor with distaste.

150 years and not a damn thing changed.

The Summer Palace had once been a place of delicate beauty. The ancient texts praised its ability to bring poets to tears and inspire the people.

Those days are long past unless delicate beauty is now defined as "overly gilded Victorian brothel."

There was nothing delicate or inspiring about the Summer Palace anymore. It was garish and gilded and tired.

Gold inlay in the floors, pearl and diamond accents in the doorknobs. Even the candlesticks in the washroom were made of platinum. *Nothing was too much for the King of the Leprechauns.*

"We guard the gold, boyo. Why shouldn't we look like we know the job?"

My father's smug voice echoed in my brain, making me want to kick the shit out of something. The King of the Leprechauns would rather die than let anyone think he was poor. Hoarding wealth and displaying it were the only things he cared about.

Two guards appeared out of a side chamber and did a visible double-take when they saw me.

"Prince Odhran? You've returned?" one of them asked, stepping forward to give me a curt bow.

I inclined my head in acknowledgement. "Not by choice, Torquil. Where is my father?"

The two guards exchanged an uneasy glance with each other and then pointed to the Council Chambers. *Great. The whole bloody council. This should be fun.*

"He's - he's in a meeting right now. Perhaps you could see Her Royal Highness Princess Eimear first and then come back?" Torquil mumbled.

I clapped him on the back and strode forward, a murderous look on my face. "Where's the fun in that? But do me a favor, send word to my sister that I'm here."

I didn't wait for a response. I gripped the double-door handles and threw them open and walked in to face the one man with big enough balls to kidnap me off a beach.

"Hello, Father," I greeted him, stomping into the room. Without waiting to hear his reply, I spied an empty chair at the center. I walked over to it, plopped down and put my feet up on the table.

"You rang?"

Gasps of surprise, outrage and fear filled the room as the rest of the Council eyeballed me warily.

My father flushed several shades of red that clashed horribly with his hair. *He looks like a tomato left out in the sun too long.*

"You forget yourself, Odhran," he hissed, slamming his palm down on the table and making several courtiers jump.

I shrugged and drew circles on the table with my finger, the picture of boredom.

"Guards!" he called out, jabbing his finger in Torquil's chest before pointing at me. "Take my worthless son out of this chamber and restrain him in the dungeons until I decide to deal with him."

Torquil swallowed heavily and crept towards me. I gave him a feral grin and stood.

"That won't be necessary, father. I have the information you seek right now. Have me taken away and you will never know the fate of the *Anam Cara*."

The room exploded in excited chatter like a bomb went off. Which, it had.

Council members talked over each other and my father sat down in his throne heavily.

I smiled at him snidely and waved Torquil away. There was a time when I feared my father and his ire, but no longer.

I'd learned a lot in my time away. The same rules I used when dancing in the Club applied to dealing with my father: leave them wanting more.

"Well, boy? Where is it? The *Anam Cara* you claim to have knowledge of?" My father was livid and barely holding onto his self-control. *Excellent.*

It was fascinating to me.

King Blaine of the Leprechauns, completely wrong-footed. I wished I had my phone so I could memorialize this moment for all history.

"You know, your goons took me off a beach this morning. It's basically my honeymoon. I found my True Mate while I was away." I mentioned, motioning for Torquil to bring me a whiskey from the cart in the corner.

"What nonsense is this? True Mates are myths." my father spluttered, his red face growing more crimson by the moment.

The rest of the Council looked intrigued. Councilwoman Bertie leaned forward in interest.

"A True Mate? We've not had a True Mate in centuries. Fate has blessed you, Your Highness."

I grinned at the old woman and raised my glass in cheers. Bertie always was one of the good ones.

"Fate has indeed blessed me. I have gained a True Mate and a pod with brothers since I've been away."

"The. Anam. Cara." My father demanded, slapping away the courtier who tried to bring him some water. "Where is it?!"

"Do you know the origin story behind the *Anam Cara*, Father? It's really quite fascinating," I began, weighing my options in my mind. Losing the artifact would be a heavy blow, but there just may be a way to get out of getting all the blow back.

"The *Anam Cara* was the first gold piece, yes? The one Fate gifted to our great Queen Finola when she was just a wee lass. It came with the promise of riches beyond all measure." Bertie looked around at the rest of the Council to a sea of nods and murmurs. Every child in our world knew this story.

"*Anam Cara*. It's an interesting word for a piece of gold, isn't it, Father? Why would Fate give our dearly departed Queen a piece of gold as her soulmate? That's what *Anam Cara* is, isn't it? Soulmate."

"Stop this rubbish this instant and tell us whether you have the cursed thing!" Father exploded, spittle flying out of his mouth and all over the table.

"I do not have it, Father. But I know where it is. And if you want to know, you'll listen to my story. After all, you were the one who sent your goons to kidnap me off the beach on my honeymoon."

Bertie and a few of the other Councilmembers looked chagrined and mumbled apologies.

"Do you remember what happened to Queen Finola?" I asked, toying with the condensation on my whiskey glass.

"Uh, she founded The Hill and lived here with her consorts and built great riches for the Leprechaun people?" Councilman Tyrone looked around for verification.

"Her... consorts. Yes. She had several according to the history books?"

"What the blasted hell does Queen Finola's consorts have to do with anything?! You are trying my patience, boy!" Father warned, draining his whiskey glass in one swallow and throwing it against the wall.

We all watched it shatter, the pieces sliding down and scattering like glittery diamonds all over the floor.

"She was alone before she received the *Anam Cara*. Yet, Fate blessed her with four True Mates. Her consorts. Together, they ruled over our little Hill and they, and our people, prospered."

Bertie sighed, "Aye, we know the story, Your Highness. Fate smiled at us that day. But the history means nothing if we dunna have the coin. Without the gold, Fate does not smile upon us."

I stood up and paced in front of the ornate table. This was the part I had to get right. Not only for my sake, but for Kalena and the rest of our pod.

"What if the *Anam Cara* was not a gift from Fate to enrich us with gold and silver and money?" I asked, looking at each of our Council members. "What if it was something even more precious?"

Father looked so exasperated I thought he might actually fall over in disgust, but the rest of the room was hanging on to my every word. They had all known me since I was a boy, and I could feel a sense of fondness radiating from them.

"And what is more precious than the gold, eh? We are *Leprechauns.* Gold is our life. Our legacy. Our *birthright.*" My father sighed.

"Oh aye, we love our gold." I grinned and pulled a few pieces of my own to dance through my fingers. "But Fate knew that when she created this *Anam Cara*. She knew we would need something more than just gold. Gold doesna keep your bed warm at night, does it Tyrone?" I tossed a coin at him and he caught it, grinning.

"Counting gold doesna fill the days with joy and laughter, does it Bertie?" I tossed a coin at the old woman and she nodded thoughtfully.

"The *Anam Cara* is more than just gold. It's a gift from Fate for the one thing that money can't buy." I leaned over the table and waited until all eyes were on me.

"It's one of the sacred Matestones."

The room was silent for a full second before the chattering started. It was quiet at first, escalating into a dull roar.

Some believed me. I could see it in their eyes. Others looked skeptical. My father mostly looked pissed.

I sipped my whiskey and watched as the Council meeting completely went to shambles. My father glared at me from the opposite side of the room, but I just smiled. *Your move, asshole.*

King Blaine stood and raised his hands for quiet.

"It is a delightful story, is it not? A single coin gifted to our first Queen that allowed her to find those whom she was fated for. Her consorts to build our kingdom with. But that is all it is. *A story.* If the *Anam Cara* really was a Matestone, why has no other ruler found a True Mate in the centuries that we've had it since Queen Finola passed on? Why now? What proof do we have?"

I took a deep breath and set my glass on the table. *Moment of truth time.*

"I know it's a Matestone, Your Majesty, because Fate chose my mate to carry it. That Matestone brought us, my whole pod, together."

My father's face broke into a slow, triumphant smile.

"And how did she gain such a thing, my son? How did she come across our *Anam Cara*? Shall I dispatch Glen and Georgie to fetch her and ask?"

My stomach clenched. There was no way I would ever let my Father get his grubby paws in Kalena.

"She found it... in my pot of gold." I finally answered.

The Council erupted again, shouting accusations of theft and treachery that bounced off the walls. But I didn't hear any of it. I stared my father down. Even when the guards flanked me, pulling me into custody, I refused to break eye contact.

"Prince Odhran, Lord of Malloy, Guardian of the Gold, and Heir to the Hill. You are charged with grievous crimes against your people and theft. The Council will meet and decide on an appropriate sentence. These crimes must be deemed unforgivable. For a member of the Founding Families to behave in such a manner — an example must be made."

He crashed the gavel down, and Torquil and Garrett led me away.

I strained against them, but their grip was too tight and the sympathy once found in Torquil's eyes was gone.

We hurried through the secret hallways of the palace, descending deeper and deeper until we stopped before the cells.

"In you go, Your Highness," Garrett pushed me hard, and I whirled around to hit him again but Torquil held up his bat to stop me.

"Never would have thought you were a traitor, Prince Odhran. Guess it goes to show."

He slammed the door shut, plunging me into darkness.

I reached out across the matesbond that pulsed in my chest and sent love to Kalena.

Time for Plan B.

Chapter Twenty
Kalena

I knew two things.

1. Someone stole Belfast. They fucking *stole my mate.*
2. The coin I had traded for my freedom and life had somehow come back to me.

Beyond that? Nothing made sense.

My skin buzzed with anxiety as I paced the beach, replaying everything in my mind. Frank trailed a short distance behind me. The heat of the day beat down on us, but my skin felt cold from the fear. *Who would violently steal Belfast? And why?*

When they saw me screaming on the beach, Chuck and Frank had acted quickly.

Chuck whipped through the water in his dolphin form, tearing across the waves in search of our Kraken friend.

Belfast had shared little with me about his life before he left the Leprechaun hill. He kept promising that he would, but it never really came up. All I knew was that he didn't get along with his father. His proper name was Odhran, and he had *acquired* the Matestone or *Anam Cara* as he called it, before he left.

"We'll get him back, love. Just you wait and see." Frank growled. "He's Pod."

"What do you know about Leprechauns and Faery?" I asked, digging my toe in the sand and hugging my arms to myself.

"Not much, to be honest. Always thought the Fae tended to be little shitstains most of the time. I know the basic rules, like be careful with deals and such. Leprechauns are supposed to be special kinds of assholes with money, but that's all."

I laughed out loud at my grumbly mate describing all of Faery as "little shitstains."

"They beat him, Frank. They hit him over the head and dragged him away from me. How can we beat them at their own games? How do we get him back? How do we even manage a trip to Faery, of all places?"

"You need a guide."

My skin prickled, and I whirled around to see Bill sitting in a beach chair in a teeny-tiny yellow swimsuit that left absolutely nothing to the imagination. He gave me a brief wave and set his tropical drink down on a gilded table that was sort of... smoking. My inner koala actually growled. *I am going to be in therapy for so long after this.*

"What? How? *When* did you get here?" I pinched the bridge of my nose. *Bill was fucking weird and kind of scary.*

"Oh, I'm here, there and everywhere, pet. You'll get used to me. But if you'd rather.... I can leave and not tell you about Faery. I can go. It's really no bother. Morning sun isn't the best for my complexion, anyway. I prefer a steady diet of afternoon hellfire."

My shoulders slumped, and I rubbed my eyes tiredly.

He got up to pack up his beach chair, but I held out my hand in protest.

"No. I'm sorry. Please. We need help."

Bill inclined his head and sat back down. I did my best not to look at his... swimsuit. But it was proving exceedingly difficult when it kept changing colors.

Grimacing, I shook my head to clear it and tromped over to the sand where he was perched.

He smiled benignly at me and waved his hand, conjuring up matching beach chairs for Frank and I.

"Beverage?" he asked solicitously. "Sunscreen? Maybe your bear in something skimpy?"

His eyes twinkled when he looked at Frank and waved his hand again. A poof of black smoke covered Frank from head to toe for a moment. When it drifted away, I clapped my hand to my mouth.

Frank was dressed in an equally tiny purple swimsuit, the fabric straining against his bulging manhood. Glittery purple tassels covered his nipples and a flowy, lavender robe decorated his shoulders.

"What the actual *fuck*, Bilexphiles?" Frank roared, clawing at the tassels, trying to get them off. I giggled despite myself, and Frank shot me a wounded look.

"Do you like purple?" Bill turned to me and asked. He tapped his finger on his chin. "I could also do green. The big, burly men always look good in green."

He snapped his fingers again and Frank roared as the smoke came back.

I stared wide-eyed as my enraged mate appeared again, this time in an old-timey green swimsuit and swim cap. Across his calves were sock garters, and he had a small walking stick in his hand that he was clutching like a club.

Bill studied him seriously.

"You know, I just don't like vintage on him? I thought it

would work but it just.. doesn't. Third times the charm."

I gaped at him, trying to understand what the actual fuck was happening.

Before I could manage a scathing reply, Bill waved his hand again and reached for his tropical drink and sipped it daintily through the bright yellow straw. *Confusing-ass demon.*

Frank's roar sounded more like his bear, and I worried that we might push him too far.

This time, when the smoke cleared, Frank was fuming. His swimsuit had changed to the tightest pair of boxer briefs I'd ever had the pleasure of seeing. They fit him like a glove. The red buffalo plaid weirdly worked for him, as did the buffalo plaid bow tie. Bulky brown boots and thick woolen socks completed the outfit.

I couldn't stop staring. Frank looked... completely pissed off and utterly delicious.

"Right," I tore myself away from eye-fucking my delicious flannel-covered mate and turned back to Bill. "I think we can focus maybe on Belfast and getting him back? And can someone please explain to me *why* this Matestone just found me again"

Bill put his drink down and steepled his fingers together. His posture was that of a mob boss on vacation.

"Well, you are the guardian of said Matestone, dear. Where else would it be? And yes, you have a problem with your little Leprechaun. Did he, by chance, tell you his relationship to his Leprechaun family before he was... transported?"

"You mean, before he was kidnapped off this beach? No. No he did not." I snapped, the worry rising in me all over again.

Bill narrowed his eyes at me and then looked out at the peaceful sea.

"Ah! Moray joins us. Let's meet the scaly bastard,

shall we?"

I huffed in annoyance and grabbed Frank's hand. Together, we stomped back through the sand to the water's edge and waited as two water-logged figures made their way up from the sea.

Chuck stopped when he saw Frank's outfit and his eyes widened.

"Oh my goddess, what *happened* while I was gone?!"

"Dolphins favor blue, don't they?" Bill asked innocently, looking Chuck over with interest.

Before I could stop him, he had snapped his bloody fingers once more, and the smoke covered my mate. When Chuck emerged, he was dressed in board shorts covered in brightly colored fish. He had a red bucket hat on and a bright yellow inflatable floatie around his waist.

Frank let out a short bark of laughter and we trooped back to the informal circle of chairs that Bill had built.

"I am so sorry that this happened, Kalena," Moray said formally, sitting stiffly on one of the beach chairs.

"I just want him back. If I have to drag him from Faery myself."

Bill stretched and yawned loudly. "If you wanted to go to Faery, you could have just asked me. I can portal you in and out in a jiff!"

Frank clenched his fists and opened his mouth as if to speak, but I cut him off.

"Why do I feel like there's a but in that sentence?" I asked suspiciously.

Bill was the picture of innocence. "You have a delightful derriere, my dear. Don't think I haven't noticed," Both Chuck and Frank shot up and looked murderous. Bill laughed and waved them down. "However, as delectable as your rear is… that's not what I am interested in."

Moray fixed a dark look on him, and Bill shrugged.

"Think of this like a business decision. I have what you need to get your mate back, and in return, you'll give me something."

I was horrified.

"Do you - are you actually asking me for *sex* as payment to get my mate back? That's disgusting."

I moved to stand between my mates and they both draped their arms over me protectively.

Bill had the grace to look stricken. "No! Of course not. I would never... you're a mated woman, after all. And besides.. I just... No. You don't have to worry about that."

His apologetic tone did nothing to mollify me, and I felt my magic rising, eager to escape.

"My dear Miss Montague. You are a mystery, aren't you? Half-shifter, half-witch. You can access both sides of your nature now that Moray's little ritual was completed. You were chosen by Fate to guard a Matestone. You have built a pod that spans the elements."

When I didn't react, he continued.

"Your dolphin shifter is of the sea, or water. Your bear is of the land, or earth. Your Leprechaun travels by rainbow, or the air. And you, my dear, are fire. The fire of magic flows through you."

"What's your point?" I asked grumpily.

"My *point*," he stressed, "is that you are a mystery. A mystery I very much want to solve. All I need from you is a drop of your essence and I shall chauffeur you around as much as you like for the next 24 hours. We can go to Faery, we can go to France, I will even magick your mates into new underpants... my portal would be yours to command."

"Really, Bilexphiles?" Moray asked, rolling his eyes before turning to me.

"Your essence is like... the air around your soul.

Certain *creatures* can read essence and thus use it to reverse engineer a connection. It sounds creepy and you should never give your essence about casually, but I can vouch for Bilexphiles in this." Moray explained gently.

I swallowed the lump in my throat and tried to concentrate.

The air around my soul?! What the fuck is he going to do with it? Does that bind us? But when my thoughts drifted to Belfast, I knew I would give Bill my entire soul if that's what it took to get my Leprechaun back.

"How do you go about.. Acquiring my *essence?*" I asked with distaste.

Bill brightened and Moray rolled his eyes and stood, moving to the side of my mates as if preparing for them to lose their shit. *Great. Just great.*

"It's all very simple. I just need a kiss. One little kiss, doesn't need to be long and certainly no tongue. Just let me take a sample of your essence for my... Project... And away we go!"

Chuck and Frank reacted predictably.

Frank roared and partially shifted his hands. Chuck made a pained noise and stepped forward. The outfits Bill had forced them into did not aid in the desire to look fierce or foreboding. But gods, I loved them for the effort.

Moray grabbed both of their hands and held them back.

"A kiss? You want me to *kiss* you?" I asked, stepping forward, "Even though you know I have claimed my mates?"

Bill's smile was brilliant. "Yes, pet. Sometimes, a kiss is just a kiss. And, think of it as… science. A kiss for magical science if you will."

I pursed my lips together and thought about it. As far as onerous tasks went, this one was simple. Just… kiss an ancient forest demon, pop in his portal, and go save my mate.

Something in me snapped. I marched up to him and reached up, wrenching his face down towards mine. His dark black eyes glittered with interest.

"Take my essence then and get us the fuck out of here. I have to save my mate." I snapped before going up on my tiptoes and pressing a chaste kiss to the demon's lips.

To his credit, Bill just let it happen. He didn't try to touch me or deepen the kiss or take anything that I didn't freely give.

As soon as it had started, it was over. I stepped back, embarrassed and angry.

Bill touched his lips and smiled.

"I get it now. You, my dear Miss Montague, are a mystery indeed. But one I am much closer to solving. Fate has chosen her guardian well in you."

Frank growled at him again, and Moray held him back with a few murmured words.

"Your portal, my lady," Bill bowed, and a portal appeared next to him, dark black flames. Together, Frank, Chuck, Moray, Bill and I all trooped in. *Destination: Faery. Time to kick some Leprechaun ass.*

BILL'S PORTAL dumped us out in a dark room with no windows. Frank pushed to the front with Chuck behind me as we crept out into the darkness.

"Where are we?" Chuck whispered hoarsely, latching on to the back of my bikini to keep me close.

"Leprechaun Hill. Obviously." Bill answered succinctly. He moved to the side and rattled some things around until light rushed into the room, temporarily blinding us.

The window was dirty, but even with the grime, the beauty outside took my breath away. A sea of green greeted us, dotted with little cottages throughout.

"Come along! There are rules about portals in the Summer Palace and while rules rarely apply to me, I can't do anything about portal alarms." Bill ushered us through a hidden door and we spilled out into the hall.

A faint ringing sound, like the tinkling of a bell could be heard and Bill moved us along faster.

"What do you know about Belfast's father?" I asked Bill quietly.

He glanced at me and then pulled me into an alcove.

"He's not Belfast here, girlie. He's Odhran, Crown Prince of the fecking Leprechauns. You'd do best to remember that."

My breath caught in my throat. *Belfast was a Prince?! Actually royalty?!*

Bill studied my face and let out an exasperated sigh.

He pulled me back to the others. "The man you call Belfast, is actually Crown Prince Odhran. Refer to him by his title here or there will be holy Leprechaun hell on you all. The Leprechauns are the most pretentious of the UnderFae and they get very worked up by titles." he announced shortly.

Chuck and Frank looked dumbfounded, but nodded. There was nothing else we could do. I felt the irrational desire to giggle that Lucky Charmz had employed honest-to-goddess royalty as a stripper.

"Right. So his father is King Blaine, right cranky old bastard. He's got a sister, Her Royal Highness Princess Eimear. She might be more sympathetic to the cause. Let's try her first." Bill muttered to himself, glancing in the hall-ways for guards to come to investigate the portal alert.

Our footsteps sounded like thunder in the wide, empty

hall, but we still followed Bill through the maze and up staircases until we arrived at a simple door with silver filigree and pearl accents. No one questioned how Bill knew where to go. He was just... Bill. Bill had an impressive wealth of knowledge.

The door was decorated with an elaborate crest around the letter E. *E is for Eimear!*

"This is she. Let's get this over with!" Bill pushed through the door and we all trooped in.

A small, childlike scream greeted our ears, followed by a grunt of pain. I looked around in surprise to see a tiny woman wielding a bat standing over Moray.

"Uh, we come in peace. I swear. We're friends of Belf-I mean, Odhran. The Prince! Shit... uh, your brother?" I stammered, eyeing the dynamo that somehow got the jump on a legendary Kraken. She looked ready to kick some serious ass. I liked her already.

Moray laid there like a lump on the ground and I wondered if he was actually knocked out or if he was just biding his time for revenge. You never could tell with Krakens. *What even is my life?*

"Friends of Odhran?" she narrowed her eyes at me, "And just friends are ya? Who are the gents with you? Court Jesters?"

"Mate." I admitted, "Odhran is my mate. This is his pod. We're here to get him back."

She eyed all of us suspiciously before lowering her bat and motioning us to the sitting area next to an impressive fireplace.

Once we were all settled, she poured herself a drink and downed it in one gulp.

"First things. You may call me Eimear. My brother is the most important person in the world to me, and Father sees this whole thing as an excuse to get rid of the problem child. You will have an uphill battle getting to him, even I am forbidden from visiting that level of the dungeons."

Bill looked like he was about to say something, but Eimear shot him a baleful look. "*All* magic is blocked on those levels."

"If Odhran really stole the *Anam Cara*, there's not much we can do. If they prove it, the penalty is death. My father might advocate for permanent banishment, but either way he's not in the best of moods to negotiate. "

My heart clenched. Belfast/Odhran was my best friend and newly discovered mate. The idea of him dying was abhorrent.

"He didn't steal the *Anam Cara*," I protested, "I did. Well, not on purpose. Fate gave it to me and... it turned out to be a Matestone which was this whole other thing and now I have a pod and I initially lost the *Anam Cara* because my koala was broken so I had to use it to save my life. But then it came back because I guess I'm its guardian?"

Eimear froze at that. Peering at me closely, she looked like she was trying to decide which part of that to unpack first.

"Start at the beginning. It may be the only way to save my brother."

The whole sordid story poured out of me. The Lucky Charmz Club, the way my parents had suppressed my shifter side, the bet I made with Belfast and subsequent selection of gold, my car accident, meeting my mates and then fixing my koala — everything that had happened in the last several weeks tumbled out in an exhausting mess of words. It felt cathartic to tell someone and get it off my chest.

Eimear listened with rapt attention., her eyes darting between the five of us with increasing agitation

When I was finished, Eimear sat perched on the edge of her seat with a shocked expression on her face.

"This changes everything." she muttered to herself, jumping down to pace her room.

"Fate decreed... Fate chose... Fate... mated?" she continued muttering and pacing, swinging her bat in her hands.

"Belonged to Fate! That's it!"

Moray and Bill exchanged a look, and then a wide smile broke out over Bill's face. He looked at the tiny Princess with renewed respect.

"If *Fate* gave us the *Anam Cara*, *Fate* can take it away. Odhran stole it because he was *compelled to*, in order to ensure he followed his path as designated by Fate in order to find his mate. There could be no other way. To prevent it would have been to prevent Fate from carrying out her sacred mission." she said triumphantly.

"But what's saying the King won't come back and say that his capture was also Fate acting to right a wrong?" Frank asked gruffly.

Eimear brushed that aside. "You don't need to convince my father, you just need to convince the Council. Father's really more... ceremonial. The Council keeps him around because Leprechauns are suckers for tradition, but he's on a short leash with the threat of a muzzle"

"Oh, kinky!" Bill said delightedly.

Eimear looked vaguely ill at the mention of her father and the word kinky in the same sentence.

"Come, I'll take you to them. They will hold the trial and sentencing in the justice arena."

We trooped out of her room to go save my mate and fuck with the King and Council of the Leprechauns. *As one does.*

Chapter Twenty-one
Belfast

Kalena was here. I knew it as certainly as I knew my name. I could feel her presence somewhere close by. I prayed to the Moon Goddess that she was here by her own free will and not because my father's minions had snatched her, too. Anger filled me at the thought of those dickwads putting their grubby little hands on my mate.

If anyone hurts her, they die. Simple as that.

The matesbond in my chest hummed, and I concentrated on it, reaching out through the connection to caress her. Now that I understood the pull between us, I never wanted to be apart from her. The years I spent hanging out with her at Lucky Charmz as a friend were a bittersweet memory. I appreciated that I got to know her, but I wished I had found her earlier and known who she would be.

But mate or best friend or both… I had always loved her. From the moment I met her, I think a part of me recognized it.

While I never wanted her to be within the grasp of my father or the Council, that she came after me even when I was such a dick to her about the Anam Cara made my heart sing. *She loved me. Or at least liked me enough to rescue my ass before she chewed it out.*

The sound of movement outside my cell had me on high alert, and I backed away from the door warily. The key creaked as it turned in the lock and my body tensed.

"Your Highness. You have been summoned."

The guard held the door for me and I walked out, my head held high. My mate was here, and I had to survive and protect her and our pod... no matter what.

We walked silently down the narrow passageways that spiraled up to the judicial court arena where my father and his Council routinely held public trials... and executions.

Crime amongst my people was rare, but when it happened, it was dealt with harshly. The dull roar of a crowd grew louder the closer we got to the arena, and my pulse quickened.

Crowds were my specialty. I never suffered from stage fright and I knew what the people wanted. They wanted justice, sure, but they also wanted something more primal. They wanted *the story*. They wanted to feel part of something. Like there was something bigger than all of us at play.

The *Anam Cara* was a legend come to life, and it was gone. I could only hope the truth and the story behind the Matestone and our much beloved Queen would be enough to capture the imagination of my countrymen and sway the public opinion in my favor.

The ornate doors that led to the arena floor were gilded in burnished silver. I scoffed in disgust. My father had truly spared no expense in his redecorating of the Summer Palace. I wondered what the impact would have been on our people if he had bothered to share the wealth with them instead of polished door knobs for his prisoners.

My guards flanked me and they opened the door in tandem, leading me out onto the stone floor.

My Father sat smugly on his throne, his crown glimmering brighter than the sun as his people - our people - stomped and screamed from the stands.

The noise was deafening.

I glanced up, hoping to spy my sister near my Father but the smaller chair was empty and a rock of sadness settled into my chest. *Maybe it was for the best.*

The guards led me to a single wooden chair in the middle of the arena floor and shoved me roughly into it. *Show time.*

Carefully, I stood and held my hand out in protest to the guard who came to force me to sit.

"Your Majesty. I stand before you, wrongly accused." I called out clearly.

It was against protocol, but he who speaks first controls the narrative and I wanted to get out ahead of it. The crowd ate it up and my father frowned down at me, motioning lazily for the clamoring masses to cease and desist.

"Prince Odhran, do you know why you stand before us today?" his nasally voice boomed from the balcony.

I stood tall and strong.

"I have been accused of stealing the *Anam Cara*." I said clearly. The crowd booed, and I tried not to wince.

"You admitted you did such a treacherous act in front of the Council. Your guilt has already been established." My Father crowed, looking around at the unsmiling faces of the Council who surrounded him. "Do you have the artifact to present back to us and clear your name?"

I shook my head. "I do not."

"Then all we need to do is decide your fate, boy. You have betrayed your people, your station, your heritage in this selfish act. Your theft has defied Fate herself." He droned on, playing his part in the crowd with gusto. Father always loved a touch of drama.

"Is there anyone here who will speak on Prince Odhran's behalf?" He jeered, looking around.

The entire arena grew silent.

"I will." A soft clear voice broke the silence, and I held my breath. *Kalena.*

My mate, still dressed in a bikini and sarong, stepped out onto the area floor. She was flanked by my sister, the demon Bill, and my pod-mates in a very curious state of dress. *Was that Chuck in a pool floatie? What is happening?*

My sister gave me a soft smile before turning to face our father.

"Your Majesty," she began, smiling out at the crowds before us, "Like you, I was troubled by the reports that our very own Prince Odhran, my *brother,* would be involved in such an act against our people. I found it my sworn duty to investigate and I bring you additional evidence, my King."

I had to admit; I was impressed. My quiet, reserved little sister had grown a backbone while I was away. She handled our father masterfully, and the crowd leaned in to see what would happen next.

King Blaine looked lost in thought, scowling over the balcony railing at his two recalcitrant children.

"You may present your evidence, Princess Eimear, but I regret to inform you that your brother has already claimed his guilt in front of the Council this morning. Our hands are tied on the matter."

Eimear inclined her head regally and turned to my mate. I desperately wanted to reach out and hold her, apologize for my behavior and reassure her that there was nothing that would ever jeopardize my feelings for her. But the fear of what my father could do to her held me back.

Speaking softly to Bill, I saw Kalena fish a small object wrapped in a paisley bandana out of her bikini top and hand it to him. *What on earth is she planning?*

"Uh, hi. Your Kingliness. Um," Kalena stepped up and gave an awkward bow that mostly just displayed her cleavage to the Council seated in front of her. I glared at the men who leered at her, the fury in my expression promising quick and brutal retribution.

"Your Majesty, this is Kalena Montague of Misty Cove, California. She is a Matestone Guardian, chosen by Fate." Eimear interjected before pushing Kalena forward slightly.

The crowd murmured among themselves excitedly. Matestone Guardians had been widely regarded as legend. Having one appear in the middle of the justice arena was definitely big news.

My father thought so, too. He sat up and peered down at Kalena.

"You may approach, Ms. Montague," he commanded.

Kalena nervously stepped forward a few steps and stopped, craning her head to look up at him.

"What proof do you bring us that you are as you declare? A Matestone Guardian?"

Kalena swallowed hard and turned to motion Bill to come forward. He looked particularly terrifying, with long black robes and little curls of smoke coming off his horns.

He carried the paisley wrapped packet in front of him and slowly unwrapped it, revealing a small, burnished gold coin.

My breath caught in my throat, and I looked back at Kalena with questions in my eyes. She told me on the beach that it was gone. Did she lie?

Whispers raced through the arena, the sound echoing like a hiss. My father lumbered down the steps to examine the coin himself, his own heavy crown falling lopsided on his head in his haste.

Bill stood stoically, his hand outstretched with the coin laying in the middle. The smoke curling out of his horns gave him an eerie, evil look that would have given a less greedy man pause.

But not King Blaine.

My father huffed and puffed over to him and looked down at the coin in rapture.

"*Anam Cara!*" he whispered reverently. When he reached out to touch it, Bill snatched it away and passed it back to Kalena. I enjoyed the look of mottled red fury and confusion that crossed my father's face.

"The *Anam Cara* belongs to Leprechaun Hill!" he thundered, trying to reach around Bill to get to my mate. Frank growled menacingly, still capable of eliciting fear even when dressed like a lumberjack fantasy model.

"This coin was forged by Fate," Bill began, waving my father off and magicking up a much grander throne for himself to sit in.

"Any fool can see that it has the inscriptions of the ancient Leprechauns on it. For it was once given by Fate to a Leprechaun guardian. That would be your good Queen Finola. She was a lovely girl, you know. Exceptionally good at poker and had a mean left hook."

My father scoffed and threw his hands up in disgust, but Bill just raised a single eyebrow and continued on, addressing the arena.

"Once Queen Finola accepted the guardianship of this gift, do you remember what happened?" Bill looked around expectantly. A tiny child in the front row waved his hand and Bill stood and glided over to him.

"The good Queen Fin'la found her four husbands!"

Bill beamed at the boy, terrifying everyone within sight

of him. He magicked a flamboyant golden hat out of thin air and bowed, presenting it to the delighted child.

"Even your children know the story," he glided back to his throne and addressed the Council, neatly sidestepping my father.

"Upon receipt of her gift from Fate, Queen Finola found her True Mates. Her consorts. Do you think that happened by coincidence? What are the odds that her four consorts, from four different parts of Faery, would one day converge on Leprechaun Hill to win the heart of your Queen?"

The entire arena was caught in Bill's web. He truly was a master of his craft, whatever that was.

"There are no coincidences with Fate, and Queen Finola was indeed afforded a great honor. For she, your very own *Queen*, was selected to be one of the first Matestone Guardians. Upon her death, her consorts engraved the gift with the words *Anam Cara*. It means soulmate. For they were brought to her by Fate and they loved her and stood by her side for her entire life."

Sniffles could be heard around the arena as people thought about the love Queen Finola had for her consorts and the dedication of her men to their strong Queen.

"We honor Queen Finola and her consorts. If she were also a Matestone Guardian, does that not make the theft of this Matestone even more grievous by Prince Odhran?" My father groused.

"Tell me, King Blaine, do you believe Fate makes mistakes?" Bill asked softly

My father looked around nervously. He was a greedy, money-hungry sonofabitch, but even he could see a trap that obvious.

"Of course not," he finally said heavily.

Bill brightened considerably and perched himself back

on his throne. He motioned for Kalena, Frank and Chuck to go stand next to me. Chuck's yellow duck floatie brushed against the back of my neck, and I bit back a dick joke.

"As your King has declared, Fate does not make mistakes," Bill boomed, smoke rising from his throne in an impressive plume.

"And you, people of Leprechaun Hill, are here for a historic moment. Stand, celebrate with us, for the Matestone of Queen Finola has a new Guardian. She is strong and will protect this Matestone well. Your Prince has cared for her, protected her and set her on her sacred path. She has accepted him as one of her True Mates. I must introduce to you the one, the only, Kalena Montague."

The arena burst out into thunderous applause. My father looked pale and confused, and several members of the Council had sour looks on their faces. Kalena looked shell-shocked, and I caught her arguing with Bill and gesturing to her beachwear and that of Chuck and Frank.

Bill rolled his eyes and turned to Moray to whisper something before shrugging and waving smoke towards my pod-mates and magicking them into very regal street clothing.

Eimear hugged Kalena and pushed her towards me.

I caught her and stared into her eyes for a long moment, unsure of what to say, how to even start again after everything.

"So, your dad is a dick." she said suddenly, making me burst out in laughter.

"Yes, he is." I pulled her into my embrace and held her tightly.

"I have some complaints about the way you communicate about your family, *Highness.*" she snarked in my ear.

I pulled away enough to catch her eye. "Yeah... so,

about that, technically… you're now a Princess, too. It's a whole thing."

My mate looked less than pleased by that news, but Eimear overheard and squealed in happiness. "I've always wanted a sister!"

Eimear darted off to the side of the arena and started talking animatedly with one of her attendants. Within seconds, she had a beautiful circlet in her hands and she ran back to Kalena.

"One of the best things about being a Princess is the jewelry." she said, motioning for Kalena to kneel down so she could put the circlet on her head.

"Do you just have people holding spare tiaras for you everywhere you go?" I teased my little sister.

She shot me a look that could melt a glacier. "Of course I do. Ever since someone abandoned his post, I have to do all his duties and mine."

I mumbled an apology and then turned to the cheering crowd and presented my newly crowned mate to my people.

She turned in wonder and offered the people a wave while Frank, Chuck, and I positioned ourselves around her.

I caught Bill's eye and mouthed, "Thank you," over the din. He just winked and pulled a tropical drink out of thin air for himself and Moray.

The mercurial demon and the mysterious Kraken had both taken a personal interest in Kalena and the rest of our pod, but rather than threatening, it felt protective.

I was grateful to have an all-powerful being and a mythical sea lord in our corner when the chips hit the table.

"Two questions," my beautiful mate whispered, still waving uncertainly to her adoring fans.

"One, how long do we have to stay here? Two, are there unicorns here and if so, can we see them?"

I grinned and motioned for Eimear and her guards and Bill and Moray.

"Time for us to go home," I announced. "And we need to go by the Unicorn Mountains and Pegasus Valley for Kalena to get her fix."

Eimear hugged us all, even Moray, who blushed red to the roots of his hair. *I hazard a guess that Kraken's don't get hugs very often.*

"I will visit you at this beach town you've claimed." She said fiercely, before wiping her eyes and turning away from us to attend to my father.

He was standing there all alone, looking defeated and sullen. I took a step towards him, hoping to reconcile, but he turned his back on me.

Bill clapped me on the shoulder and steered me to my mate and my pod.

"Trust me, Odhran, your true family are the ones you love, not the ones who share your blood."

With my mate in my arms and my pod at my back, I pulled open my rainbow portal and we stepped inside.

It was time to go home.

Chapter Twenty-two
Kalena

My pod hovered around me, finding excuses to touch me as we walked down the beach in a group. After escaping Leprechaun Hill and getting Belfast back, we didn't feel like being apart.

The wet sand squished against my toes, and the sea breeze cooled my skin. Misty Cove was in the middle of an unprecedented heat wave and it was scrambling my brain, giving me ideas of stripping down and running around naked.

My men. My pod. My... mates.

It was amazing how they fit so seamlessly into my life. Frank, my fierce protector. Chuck, my sweet lover. Belfast, my best friend.

I loved them. A shiver went down my spine as I realized that fact. *I. Loved. Them.*

If we were out in the world, maybe people would scoff and say it was impossible to love three men after a month. They would probably tell me I was just kidding myself. Delusional.

But I knew better.

What Fate brought together, no one would ever put asunder.

"Come on, love, we have something to show you," Frank pulled my hand towards the lighthouse tower and I hurried to stay on pace with him.

"My lady, your surprise awaits!" Chuck was waiting at the bottom of the ladder with a brilliant smile.

Belfast had already made it up the ladder and was waiting at the top, his golden legs hanging off the edge.

Cautiously, I crept up the rungs and a jolt of electricity went through me when Belfast reached down to pull me up the rest of the way. Would their touch ever stop making me feel like I was about to combust? *God, I hope not.*

Frank and Chuck followed me up and the four of us crowded on the narrow lookout, gazing out at the quiet surf.

"This is beautiful," I sighed, leaning into Frank's broad chest while my hands searched for Chuck and Belfast.

"Yes. You are." Chuck whispered huskily in my ear. I shivered again and wiggled my ass against Frank.

Belfast was leaning against the railing, looking at me with enough heat in his eyes to set the entire world on fire. Desire flooded me and I ground my ass against Frank again, harder.

We hadn't been together since I claimed them and I craved them. All of them. In as many combinations I could get. *Can you get addicted to dicks? What if you are addicted to three of them?*

I kicked my flip-flops off and untied my sarong, leaning against my men in my bright yellow bikini.

"Sweetheart, do you want to play a game?" Chuck asked. His voice was low and husky with desire. My skin broke out in goosebumps in anticipation.

"I'm down. What did you have in mind?" I answered, breathlessly.

"How about... you follow our directions to the exact letter and then we make you come until you can't stand anymore?"

My entire body came alive at the idea. *Yes. Please. Times a million.*

"I can do that," I managed. My tongue darted out to lick my lips, and I caught Belfast staring at me hungrily.

"OK. Do exactly what we say, sweetheart. If you do, we reward you. If you do not... we punish you." Chuck continued.

Punish me? Intriguing.

"What punishments are we talking about?" I asked suspiciously.

Frank pulled a little velvet bag out of his pocket and held out a small silicone egg that had a remote.

"We have our ways," he growled, pressing the remote and making the little egg vibrate violently in his palm.

I swallowed hard. *Oh yeah, this was happening.*

"Are you ready?" Belfast asked. The setting sun made him glimmer like a golden god come to life, and I eyed him appreciatively. Guys like him needed to come with a warning label. *Good thing he was all mine.*

"I sure am. Do your best, loves!"

They growled noises of approval and prowled around me, crowding me up against the wall of the lifeguard shack. A thrill ran through me. We were out of the way and up high on the lifeguard shack, but we were still in public and this was very much a public beach. Anyone could come by.

Heat curled in my belly and I leaned back against Frank and awaited my fate. *My Fate given mates.*

"Close your eyes," Belfast whispered. My eyelids fluttered shut, and I inhaled shakily. I felt so alive out here with them like this.

Frank moved from his spot behind me and I heard a scraping noise behind me and the creak of metal. My curiosity burned, and I wanted to open my eyes, but I wanted to finish the game more.

"Keep your eyes closed and take three steps backwards." Chuck ordered.

I hesitated for a brief second, remembering the creaky metal ladder that got us up here. But I knew my mates would rather die than let harm befall me.

As soon as my third step was completed, warm lips covered mine. The stubble scraping against my cheek told me it was Frank. He devoured me, his kisses demanding and possessive until I moaned into his mouth and pressed my body flush with his.

Then he was gone.

"Take four steps to your left," Belfast crooned. Fingertips danced lightly along the back of my neck and made me shiver.

One. Two. Three. Four.

The fourth step had a rough lip, and I stumbled, pitching forward with a cry of alarm. Strong hands caught me around the waist, righting me before I fell. The temperature was cooler here, and I realized they had unlocked the interior of the tower.

"Let us help you to your knees," Frank said, gently lowering my body until my knees hit something soft and plush. "We're going to blindfold you, baby."

I nodded happily. The sensory deprivation of a blindfold was unexpected and combined with a semi-public location, I felt deliciously *naughty*.

Someone carefully brushed my hair, pulling it back into

a low ponytail before a silky soft piece of fabric was tied over my eyes.

"You can open your eyes. Tell us if you can see anything through the blindfold?" Belfast ordered.

I complied, opening my eyes to the pitch darkness of the blindfold.

"Nothing to see here!" I replied cheekily, blowing a kiss in the general direction of where I thought they were. My heart thundered in my chest. Just outside our tiny booth I could hear the cheerful calls of the gulls and the gentle crashing of the waves.

Rough hands skimmed the top of my shoulders and pulled gently on the bikini top tie, loosening it until it fell forward exposing me. My nipples tightened to sharp peaks, and I inhaled sharply. I loved not knowing what was going to happen next. Thrills ran up and down my body as I knelt, waiting for them to touch me.

Strong hands curved over my ribs, reaching around from behind me and palming my breasts, tweaking my nipples until I gasped. Heat washed over me in a tidal wave of arousal.

"Hold still and do not move," Chuck instructed.

I gulped and took a deep breath, centering myself. My mates explored my body, trailing their hands all over me - caressing and stroking me until I wanted to purr like a cat and rub up against each one of them. Someone nibbled the side of my neck, pressing searing kisses to my pulse point and making me cry out. Another one took one of my nipples in his mouth, tugging gently with his teeth until a gasp escaped my lips.

The sensations built on each other, teasing me and making me tense in anticipation.

I wanted more. My hands, frozen at my side, ached to touch them. To explore their bodies and bring them pleasure. Not moving while they slowly built my pleasure up from an ember to an inferno was a special sort of torture that I was determined to win.

"You're doing so well, *a stór,* perhaps we should up the ante?" Belfast whispered, pressing a sweet kiss to the corner of my mouth. My inability to kiss him back without moving made me want to howl with frustration.

Someone moved behind me, his hands resting on my hips and toying with the ties to my bikini bottom. I told myself this was a test, that I should stay strong. But it was hard. *He was hard.*

He pulled me up against him, and my back rested against his warm, broad chest. His hard cock pressed up against the small of my back.

I whimpered and edged slightly closer, angling my body to maximize our contact before I froze in realization.

I moved. That meant I broke the rules. *Oh shit.*

"Tsk tsk, sweetheart. You didn't hold still!" Chuck admonished me playfully.

The hands and lips on my body that had driven me to such heights disappeared, leaving me bereft, blindfolded and confused.

"Time to take your punishment, *a stór,*" Belfast teased. "Lean backwards until you are flat on your back, spread your legs, and wait for us to decide what to do with you."

I did what I was told, but the anticipation threatened to kill me. They whispered together, soft enough that I couldn't quite make out what they were saying. Soft laughs and the ominous buzzing sound of the silicone egg toy made me shiver.

"Bend your knees, love." Frank trailed his work-rough- ened hands down my calves and I hastened to obey. His fingers danced along my skin, tracing the path up my inner thigh until he reached the edges of my swim bottoms. The rough pad of his finger caressed the innermost edges of the clothing, making me shiver again.

"Because you moved when we told you not to, you can't come unless we give you permission." Frank growled at me, darting a single finger under my suit and plunging it into my wetness.

I moaned. His touch was like a fire in my veins. I craved him. All of them.

"Are you ready for the toy?" he asked, his finger still pumping in and out of me.

"Yes, please," I answered, shakily.

The blunt tip of the love egg teased my entrance before sliding in, Frank's long fingers pushing it in until it was anchored. Carefully, he withdrew his fingers and scooted my suit back into place.

"Pick a number between 1 and 10," Chuck asked suddenly.

"4"

The egg inside me vibrated, pulsated in a gentle pattern that was both arousing and utterly maddening at the same time. I squirmed in protest, hoping to somehow increase the speed, but they held me down.

"What did we say, love?" Frank asked me, his hot breath tickling the inside of my ear.

"You said, I can't come until you give me permission." I panted.

"This will help you focus, *a stór*. We will be right here if you need us. Sink into this and concentrate. With each sense we take away, you will feel it even deeper. When we tap on your skin like this, you'll know you have permission."

Belfast slid headphones over my ears and I immediately heard nothing except the faint sounds of an orchestra playing.

With my eyes blindfolded and my hearing muffled, my entire body tingled. The steady, gentle vibrations of the egg rolled through me. It was a loss of control, an act of surrender to my mates, that was new and terrifying at the same time.

Hands encircled my wrists and my ankles, stroking my limbs and holding me in the spread-eagle position.

I felt exposed and vulnerable, but their soft kisses on the underside of my wrist and the nimble fingers massaging my thighs and legs, reassured me they were there. They were watching as I tumbled deeper into the pleasure they had created for me. They gave me the space to surrender my pleasure to them and trust that they would care for me as their mate.

The music rose to a crescendo, and so did the vibrations of my egg. I writhed and thrashed, fighting off the climax that was building while simultaneously longing for it. Whenever a moan escaped me, one of them captured my lips with a blistering kiss, swallowing the sound and sending licks of electricity through my veins.

They adjusted the toy with the music; the intensity ebbed and flowed with the music in the most maddening of ways. I had never felt anything like it.

My entire body was on fire with pleasure and each time I reached the precipice, they gently backed me down. Over and over, until my limbs were shaking.

"Please, please let me come," I whispered fervently.

Their hands on me stilled, and the vibrations receded slightly. Soft hands pulled my swimsuit ties and eased the soaked fabric off my quivering thighs. I bit my lip, arching my back in hopes I had earned my reward.

Firm hands on my hips pulled me forward, and I fisted my hand in the plush blanket below me. The stubble of an unshaved jaw rasped against my inner thigh, and my back arched in response to his touch. Wet heat flared between my legs and I trembled in desire.

When his hand finally touched me, sliding so gently between my legs, I cried out, almost losing myself when the first broad sweep of his tongue caressed my clit.

Even with two of my senses locked away, I knew who they were. I could feel our connections pulsing between us, driving us to new heights together.

Frank ate me out, his tongue working its magic while the egg continued its mission to drive me to the brink of passing out. His beard brushed against my inner thigh and made me tingle with each pass. Belfast lay beside me, his hard body pressed up against mine as he kissed me deeply. His long fingers framed my face, and each kiss felt like a lifetime of promises.

Chuck lay pressed along my other side, his thick erection pressed firmly up against my thigh. He nuzzled my neck, nibbling my pulse point while his fingers roamed, caressing my breasts and tweaking my nipples until the sensation was almost too much to bear.

My body begged for release as my mates expertly drove me higher and higher. The music got louder and their caresses more frantic. The vibrator speed increased and Frank teased my clit until it was so sensitive I thought a light breeze might set me off.

As the music eased into the final crescendo, my body tightened. All three of them tapped lightly on my skin, giving me permission to finally, finally fall off the edge.

I screamed as my orgasm rocked through me, shattering my senses and curling my toes as wave after wave crashed over me. I thrashed and writhed next to them, every inch of me alive in sensual energy.

Strong, gentle hands stroked my body, cooling the heated skin and holding me as I came down. The egg was eased out of my pulsating sex and the headphones and blindfold gently removed.

Each of my mates kissed me, whispering their secret messages of love and desire in my ears, promising me a lifetime of happiness.

They draped themselves over me, content to hold me as I lay spent on the floor of the lighthouse shack, sex drunk and happier than I ever thought I'd be in my entire life.

The Matestone glimmered from where it had fallen on the floor, and I smiled. Fate found each of us, from the pole at Lucky Charmz to the side of the road in the Mojave Desert to the beachside mechanic shop in Misty Cove and brought us together.

Happily Ever After was only the beginning.

Epilogue
Kalena - Six Months Later

L ife in Misty Cove was nothing short of idyllic. After everything had settled, my Pod and I had taken an extensive vacation to... get to know one another. Naked. Belfast surprised us all with his very diverse property portfolio, and we spent a glorious month island-hopping through the Caribbean. Three weeks of never-ending pina coladas and orgasms with just my mates was exactly what we needed.

We returned home to Misty Cove, loved-up, suntanned and sex-drunk and ready to start our new life. The community was nothing short of welcoming and, for the first time in my life - I felt like I belonged.

Moray offered me a job as a receptionist at his shop. He claimed it was because he wanted to spend more time at sea, but more often than not he was lurking in the corner and soaking up all the knowledge I could pass on about computers and technology. I spent just as much time trying to explain pop culture references as I did answering the phone. Cthulhu was of particular concern to him as he sought to understand humans better.

As I revamped his marketing campaign and started

booking more charters, he came out of his shell more and more. Before we knew it, Misty Cove Marina & Charters was operating at full capacity, all day, every day.

We celebrated by getting him his very first smartphone. He celebrated by dropping it to the bottom of the sea when the alarm went off and disrupted his naptime.

The Kraken had officially joined the modern world. Mostly.

Chuck went back to work at the mechanic shop. His membership in Sea Lion MC was reduced to part time, and Earl and Trevor even gave him his own service bay at the shop to work on his new project: custom motorcycles.

Being the only two fated pods around, we all spent a lot of time over at the Sea Lion Clubhouse and Buoy 6 hanging with Ronnie and her guys. There was something to be said about hanging with people who just... got it. You couldn't fight Fate. And we didn't want to.

Frank expanded his trucking business into short-haul runs and hired a few more drivers to keep up the long-haul business without him. I loved having him home almost every night. He spent months researching koala shifters and painstakingly built a "Shifters 101" course that we dutifully went through each weekend together. The more I connected with my koala and practiced shifting, the better I felt.

And Belfast? Belfast started an all-male revue in Misty Cove that opened to a packed audience and brought in supes from all over the West Coast. He recruited Chuck as a dancer for special occasions and installed a permanent pole on our party deck for "practice." There was never a shortage of glitter in our house, or our lives. He still got up on stage periodically to keep his skills fresh, but all his private dances belonged to me... and occasionally Chuck.

Our days were busy, discovering new things and

working within our community, but our nights were reserved for our pod. We grew as individuals and as a unit.

I often took a walk down the beach and marveled at the way life had worked out. In one brief span of time, I had not only found my true self— but I had also found my true mates, a place to put down roots, a community of friends that felt like family, and my calling as a Matestone Guardian.

The End

Author's Note

Dear Reader,

Thank you so much for picking up this book and giving it a chance. *All That Glitters* was a labor of love and ridiculousness, like every book in this series. It also fought me and forced me to delay my original release date. What can I say? If you are going to commit to writing a Koala-witch, a Leprechaun prince who moonlights as a stripper, a grumpy Grizzly, and a diehard romantic dolphin... you want to get it right.

I hope it was everything you wanted. Please consider leaving a review so others can find this series. Indie authors are little fish in a big pond, and reviews/recommendations make a tremendous difference. Love it, hate it — I want to hear your honest review.

Did you find a typo? Ugh. Sorry about that. This book went through a lot of eyes before it got to you but sometimes those little buggers are sneaky. Please, please don't report it to Amazon. Just send me a note at emeraldfernpress@gmail.com and I'll make sure it gets updated.

What's next? When's the next book?

My *Matestone Guardians* world is very dear to me. This whole quirky, ridiculous world started last summer with *Surf's Up* after a very bizarre dream about sea lion shifters. With the pandemic raging around us and worry and anxiety dogging our every move, I wrote that book in a month and hit publish. The Matestone Guardians series was born.

Right now, this series of interconnected standalones has seven books planned. *All That Glitters* is book 2 and *Birds of a Feather* is planned for later this summer. I do not have release dates for the future iterations set in stone but my goal is to release a new Matestone book every quarter until the series is complete. Each book can be read standalone but some characters make cameos in each book so it might be helpful to start at book 1.

Wanna be the first to hear of new Matestone news and other titles I have coming out? I release a title roughly once a month.

Join my monthly newsletter: sendfox.com/beemurraybooks and come hang out in Book Club on Facebook. facebook.com/groups/beemurraysbookclub or follow me on Instagram: @BeeMurrayBooks

Author's Note

Thank you so much for reading! Keep scrolling and get a sneak peek of one of the harem members in *Birds of a Feather*.

 Bee

Also by Bee Murray

Contemporary Romance Standalones

Smexy Men & Fierce Women. Steamy Romance. Also writes under C.J. Cartwright

Quarantined Hearts

Steamy BDSM M/M/F - Menage

Kissing Mr. Perfect (co-written with C.J. Vincent)

Steamy friends-to-lovers M/M

Coming This Fall: Malicious Compliance (Men of the C-Suite Series)

Steamy Brat-Taming Billionaire M/F , writing as C.J. Cartwright

Matestone Guardians Series

PNR Reverse Harem/Rom Com Interconnected World

Surf's Up

All That Glitters

Birds of a Feather (Summer 2021)

Twice Shy (Fall 2021)

Pisces Paranormal PR Agency Series (co-written with Niobe Marsh)

Urban Fantasy/Paranormal Vampire Thrillers

Bad Blood: A VamPR Nightmare

Double Stakes: A VamPR Gamble

Underworld Hijinks Series

Quirky Paranormal Romance/Mythology Interconnected World (Novellas)

Calypso Springs *(M/F Hades & Persephone)*

Hell's Angel *(M/F Demon/Angel)*

Reaper's Last Homecoming *(Reaper Reverse Harem)*

About Bee Murray

Bee Murray is a die-hard romantic based out of the Pacific Northwest. An International & USA Today bestselling author and owner of Emerald Fern Press, Bee dreams of everything from grand adventures with complex characters to pun-filled romantic comedy, weird paranormal situations, extra steamy romance, and fresh ways to tell old stories. Don't expect any love triangles here, Ms. Murray is a big fan of ethical non-monogamy and it comes out in her menage romance and reverse harem stories! She writes under several pen names, including Bee Murray and C.J. Cartwright. Check out her work at beemurray.com.

Up Next: Birds of a Feather

Need more Matestone Guardians? Wanna see a little more of... Moray?

Birds of a Feather is coming this summer!
    mybook.to/Matestone3

Join my Book Club on Facebook for exclusive sneak peeks and content from Matestone Guardians!
    Facebook.com/groups/BeeMurraysBookClub

This summer, take a walk on the wild side and return to Misty Cove and the third installment of the hilarious fated mates series, Matestone Guardians.

Are you ready for the sexy adventures of a dedicated scientist, a French fry-obsessed seagull shifter, a love-lorn penguin, and a mythical sea monster who is in way over his head?

Get ready to laugh and fall in love with quirky shifters and fated mates in Birds of a Feather!

Lovers of quirky romantic comedies, #WhyChoose romance, fated mates, questionable choices, unusual shifters, and bottomless pina coladas will love this third installment in the Matestone Guardians world. And if you haven't been introduced… it's about time.

Made in the USA
Columbia, SC
12 November 2021

48739455R00150